Amanda Running Scared

Georgina Sellwood

Copyright 2015 Georgina Sellwood
ALL RIGHTS RESERVED
Cover Art by Joan Alley
Editing by Jacqueline Hopper

This book is a work of fiction and any resemblance to persons, living or dead, or places, events or locales is purely coincidental. The characters are the product of the author's imagination and used fictitiously.

Warning: The unauthorized reproduction or distribution of this copyrighted work is illegal. No part of this book may be scanned, uploaded or distributed via the Internet or any other means without the permission of Prism Book Group. Please purchase only authorized editions and do not participate in the electronic piracy of copyrighted material. Thank you for respecting the hard work of this author.

Published by Prism Book Group
ISBN-13: 978-1512162202
ISBN-10: 1512162205
First Edition, 2015
Published in the United States of America
Contact info: contact@prismbookgroup.com
http://www.prismbookgroup.com

CHAPTER ONE

Run! Get away!

The man's hands bit into Amanda Vanderbilt's upper arms as she struggled and spat at his face, to no avail. The man wore a ski mask, but the opening around his eyes let her see the shape and color of them and how his thick, black eyebrows met above the bridge of his nose.

"Shut up and come with me," her attacker growled. Her face stung where he'd hit her.

At the back of the garden, no one at the party would hear her. To scream was useless. Tears of frustration ran down her face as dance music floated on the wind.

"Let me go," she yelled in desperation. What else could she do? She'd tried all the defensive moves she knew—kicking, biting, spitting, and there was only one thing left. She would have to hurt him.

She lifted her knee high and hard. The man fell like a stone, groaning and holding himself. Her blouse ripped as he grabbed at her on his way down.

"I'll find you, Amanda. You can't hide. I know where you and the doctor lived and I know you are living with your mother now," he yelled.

The light from a street lamp shone through a gap in the hedge. She dove and crawled through the hole on hands and knees. Branches scraped her arms as dew from the grass ruined her clothes. She hobbled out of the hedge and struggled to cross the dark lawn on her broken shoe.

Was he coming? The hedge shook behind her. She gained her balance and hobbled on.

When she made it to the sidewalk, the broken heel of her Italian sandal clattered on the pavement. Her hand trembled when she raised her arm as she hailed an approaching New York cab. *Thank heavens*, it'd just pulled out of a driveway two doors away.

Footsteps pounded the ground behind her.

When the car stopped, she dove into the sanctuary of the backseat, holding the ripped pieces of her yellow silk blouse together. "Go," she screamed, slamming the door and locking it.

Her breath came in ragged gasps while her head spun. The scent of citrus cologne lingered in the enclosed space, making her want to gag.

She met the cabbie's wide-eyed stare in the rearview mirror. "Are you all right, lady?"

All right? Far from it. Who was that man who'd attacked her at the party? Kneeing him had given her the seconds she'd needed to get away. Her heart thudded against her ribs, and terror still gnawed at her nerves.

A week ago, she'd received the party invitation from a friend.

"Who's that from?" her mother had asked, nodding at the scented, pink paper Amanda held in her right hand.

"Karin Rockefeller."

"Well, surely you're not going to refuse another one. You have to stop sitting around here moping and start getting out again. Brad was killed two years ago, and it's time you get over it."

Pain had stabbed Amanda's heart after her mother's insensitive remark. Depression had descended like a shroud, enveloping her. Didn't her mother realize how much it hurt to lose her husband and move into her parent's house with her three-year-old toddler, Monica? She had felt like a dog coming back with its tail between its legs. Did anyone her age return home to their mother?

She'd been in a fog of pain for—was it really two years?

She knew she had to make the effort. Get out and be active again. Karin's party would be a good place to start. She wouldn't know too many people there, and she wouldn't have to put up with the gazes full of pity that she hated so much.

"You're right, Mother. I'll e-mail her today and accept."

"Good. We'll leave Monica with Consuela and I'll take you to Fifth Avenue to shop after lunch."

They'd found the perfect outfit, a yellow silk blouse and a matching skirt with a ruffle at the hem.

The party happened to fall on the staff's day off and Mother was at an Arts Culture meeting, so she'd left Monica with a new babysitter. Monica had clung to her hand when Amanda dropped her off. For the last two years, she'd been by Amanda's side almost constantly. Amanda had to pretend she didn't see the tears gathering in her sweet baby's eyes as she closed the door and walked to the waiting cab.

The driver sent another concerned glance over his shoulder, bringing her back to the present. "Lady, are you okay?"

"Yes." The quiver in her voice made her sound far from convincing. "Go. Just go." She swallowed, tamping back the tears that stung her throat and intensified, threatening to overwhelm her. As she bit her lip, fear beat in her chest and wouldn't be controlled as easily as her urge to cry. She looked back. A shadowy figure broke through the hedge.

The gearshift clunked as they pulled away from the curb into the overcast night. The man, still bent over and holding himself, staggered after them. He chased the car a few steps, then stumbled and fell.

"Where to, miss?"

Where should she go? Certainly not home. The attacker knew where she lived. His last words haunted her. *I'll find you, Amanda. You can't hide. I know where you and the doctor lived, and I know you are living with your mother now.*

Who wanted to hurt her? Obviously it had to be someone who knew her if he knew her address.

Her stomach rolled—she was going to be sick. She clutched at her chest and tried buttoning her blouse. It didn't help, it was ruined. Ripped and stained. Anyone who saw her would know there'd been a struggle.

The cabbie's hard gaze met hers in the rear view mirror. "Miss, I need an address. Where do you want to go?"

What should she do? Where could she go? Anywhere but to the police. When her husband had died, they'd put her at the top of the list of suspects, grilling her for months until her nerves nearly shattered. They still hadn't found his killer, and if she brought this attack to their attention, they might resume interrogating her. As far as she knew, no one at the party had seen it happen, and the police were unlikely to put out an all-points bulletin for an unknown man wearing a ski mask.

She let out a frustrated sigh, trying to clear her confusion. She wouldn't impose on her friends and relatives. What if she put them in danger? She couldn't go home or stay in town. The attacker might be anyone, and he was coming after her. She clasped her hands to control their trembling. She wanted her toddler, Monica, with her, but that would be selfish and dangerous.

Amanda hadn't been at the Rockefellers' party long when a man had bumped into her. He'd bent to pick up her clutch and apologized for knocking it out of her hand. When he'd handed it back, his dark, empty eyes had set alarm bells ringing, but she'd ignored them.

She had thought her friends would be interested in reconnecting with her after her extended absence, but when she walked to the edge of several groups, they'd ignored her and kept talking amongst themselves. They had seemed indifferent to her wanting to reintegrate. It hurt. Maybe she had been out of their circle too long, or they were just too self-centered and spoiled to notice her.

The realization had hit her hard. She'd needed to get away before someone noticed the tears that were gathering and close to spilling. She walked to the end of the garden where she knew there was a three-person swing with a bench seat.

It'd turned out to be a bad decision, because that's when the masked man had pulled her into the bushes. Thank goodness, she'd thought to use her knee.

She needed to get away to safety so she could make a plan.

"Do you want me to just drive around, or are you gonna give me an address?"

What about Monica, her little three-year-old angel? Much as she would have loved Monica to be with her, it was better to leave her where she was safe. No one would think of her being with her friend, Kate's, babysitter. Monica had never stayed with Barb before. Not even Amanda's mom would know to search for her there. Kate let Barb watch her children all the time, so she must be loving and reliable.

"Okay. Take me…umm, to the hotel on the highway," she murmured, tasting the salt of her tears.

"It's a bad time of night to be goin' there and it's gonna take a while."

Amanda brushed at her expensive clothes, trying but unable to remove the dirt and grass stains. "Yes, but I have to get out of here. Will you drive me somewhere out of town?"

"Lady, it's almost midnight. My shift is over soon. I can't."

Fresh tears stung the back of her eyes. An impossible situation. "Then, please…drop me at the nearest hotel out on the interstate."

"Okay, miss, but that'll cost you. I hope you know what you're doin'."

To pay the cabbie, Amanda peeled off a couple of bills from the meager cash in her diamond-studded clutch purse. She'd only taken enough money to get home.

"Stay safe. Don't do nothin' stupid." The cabbie shook his head one last time before driving away.

Stay safe. It wouldn't be easy. Gravel pelted her legs as he gunned the engine and sent the yellow cab streaking out of the lot and down the highway, leaving her alone in the hotel's parking lot.

Opening her wallet again, she counted the bills. Not enough for the hotel. What was she going to do?

The sound of rumbling engines caused her to turn. Fear hitched her breath as she faced a multitude of parked tankers and semis. They appeared monstrous in the tinted lights of the truck stop next door. The echo of their engines and the stench of diesel brought to mind the scary, shape-shifting toys from her childhood.

Through the window, she saw two truckers sitting at the counter in the café. She shivered in the cold. Though tempted to order something hot to drink, she decided against it, not wanting to face their reactions to her torn and soiled clothes. Glancing in the direction of town, Amanda wondered if the masked man had recovered enough to hunt for her.

Would he look here? No, of course not, but she needed to find a safe way out of the area.

A truck with a horse trailer stood at the card-lock gas pump at the edge of the lot next to the hotel. She hobbled toward it on her broken sandal. She loved horses. Dreamed of living outside the city and having one of her own to ride someday. She thought if she could just pet one…

When she drew near, she saw there were no horses inside. Disappointment saddened her.

A hunky cowboy with tanned skin and a handsome face started washing the windshield of the truck. She ducked along the far side of the trailer where he wouldn't notice her.

Darkness shrouded this side of the animal carrier. She slipped along beside the horse stalls. This one—the type owners took to competitions, staying in them while they showed their horses—had living quarters at the front.

Unable to stop her body shaking and teeth chattering, she looked to the RV part of the trailer as a warm place, out of the chilly night air. She tried the handle and it clicked open. A wave of relief washed over her.

Just then, the cowboy, his black Stetson slung low shadowing his eyes, sauntered to her side of the truck to finish washing the window. Amanda tore the door open wider and dove inside.

It was hard to see in the dim light. Her left hand rested on a three-burner stove. She had grabbed the corner of it to hoist herself inside. The dark space on the counter next to it was probably a sink. Across from her, a sofa sat along the far wall.

Footsteps shuffled in the dirt along the side of the truck. He was coming her way. In a panic, she scrambled up into the double bed on her right, at the front of the trailer.

Her breath came in ragged gasps as boots scuffed the concrete outside. She burrowed into the untidy mess of covers on the bunk, to hide if the cowboy entered. The scent of the man clung to the sheets, and she tried to regulate her breathing.

He stopped a moment then continued. Kicking the tires on his way by, he made a circuit of the truck and trailer. She took a second to catch her breath.

The truck rumbled to life and she grabbed at the sheets for support. Should she jump out or stay?

While she debated, they bumped onto the highway. They moved far too fast for her to escape. Wherever this handsome man was going, she was going, too.

She hoped she hadn't put herself in more danger by stowing away in this cowboy's trailer.

BRUCE PALMER FINISHED gassing up his boss's white pickup, did his inspection, and headed out. He tuned the radio to his favorite country music station and settled in to drive a few more hours before stopping for the night. This assignment to pick up horses on the west coast wasn't his first choice of how to spend his time. He'd rather ride fence lines or punch cows, but at least he was alone.

He didn't mind the other guys in the bunkhouse, but solitude suited him best. The only good thing about the long, cross-country drive was the alone time.

He'd taken the job at Hank Sheffield's ranch a couple of years earlier, hoping to put the past behind him. It still made him angry to think of Julia. He banged his palm on the steering wheel.

She'd tried to trick him into marrying her, telling him she was pregnant. Thank goodness, his brother, Matt, had seen through her ruse. Bruce had almost been saddled with a liar for a wife and someone else's kid to boot. The child he could handle, but her, no.

The whole thing with Julia had been bad. He wanted nothing more to do with women. All of them were trouble. They tied a man's emotions in knots and squeezed until it ached. He rubbed at his chest and blew out a large breath, releasing the tension built up inside.

Thinking of women, he'd swear he'd caught a whiff of something flowery by the RV door when he'd inspected the truck and trailer. He'd shaken his head and given the tires an extra kick.

Something about perfume and a womanly scent did things to him. Being alone might not be such a good idea. It had him longing for the soft curves of a woman. And that was asking for trouble.

AMANDA WOKE AND saw the cowboy had fallen asleep, slumped in the cab of the truck. When the man had stopped for the night, he must have been extremely tired and hadn't made it back to the trailer. She slipped the curtain closed on the window between them, crawled out of the bunk, and tiptoed to the small bathroom beyond the kitchen area.

After closing the door, she took a chance and turned on the light. A buyer's agreement on the counter showed the cowboy was going to Seattle to pick up horses. A four-day trip.

Good, she needed to get lots of distance between her and the man who wanted to hurt her. She needed to call Barb and ask her to keep Monica for an extended stay while she figured out the identity of the masked man. Amanda hoped Barb would be able to.

She flicked off the light. Afraid of tripping in the dark, she climbed back into the bunk. As she lay in the sanctuary of the bed, tucked warmly under the covers, she wondered what would happen when the cowboy found her. Would he dump her on the side of the road? In the middle of nowhere? She hoped he wouldn't be that cruel. What if he wasn't as nice as he looked?

She wasn't sure the money that remained in her clutch after paying for the cab would be enough to get by if he left her stranded somewhere. Using her credit cards must be avoided. Whoever had threatened her might be able to trace them.

She needed to check on Monica. Her three year old was constantly on Amanda's mind. If the cowboy had a cell phone, he must have it with him in the truck. She hadn't seen one in the trailer and, of course, she'd left her cell phone at home. Again. She needed to stop doing that.

There was little chance the attacker would find Monica. But what about Barb? Amanda's stomach tightened. Monica wasn't used to the new sitter. What if she was afraid of staying longer than one night? What if she made a fuss and Barb couldn't handle the toddler's tears and fussy appetite? Amanda wiped at the moisture on her cheek, but the tension in her stomach stayed.

Please, let my little angel be safe.

The back of her throat stung as she remembered what the two of them had been through since her husband, Brad, had been killed by a gunshot to the head. At first, Monica had asked constantly for her dad, tearing at Amanda's heart every time she mentioned him. Then, eventually, they settled into a new rhythm that was a little better. Now this. Sadness washed over her in waves and she fought back the tears.

Why is this happening?

CHAPTER TWO

A DOOR BANGED shut and Amanda sat up. "Monica?" she whispered.

Did her baby need her?

About to go to her, the strange blankets and odors of the trailer penetrated her sleepy brain.

Where am I? Monica isn't here. She was in the hunky cowboy's bed, safe from her attacker for now. But who was the man she'd stowed away with? He could be anybody.

Cold air pebbled her arm. He was in the trailer with her. Her arm, out from under the covers, might be seen. She pulled it back, trying not to draw his attention to the movement, praying he wouldn't find her. She needed one more day before he found her and tossed her out. The further from the city she travelled, the better she'd feel.

Water ran nearby. She peeked out. With his shirt off, the hunky cowboy stood at the kitchen sink having a wash. His bronzed skin rippled over taut muscles. Hard work had toned his physique to perfection. The cords in his forearms worked as he splashed his face. The sound of water running made her aware she needed the bathroom. She hoped the feeling would go away and he wouldn't take long.

Movement on the wall beside her caught her attention. A big, hairy spider climbed toward her and was about to get in the bed. The urge to scream built in her throat. Desperate to get up and run, she clamped her mouth shut and tried to lie still. The bug stopped and rubbed two of its legs together. Bitten on the back of the leg as a child, she knew the damage a spider bite would cause. The pain had lasted for days.

The cowboy gathered equipment to have a shave. He palmed shaving cream on the sexy day's growth on his cheeks. His sun-streaked hair shone golden where he'd sprayed water in it. He began shaving the lather away.

The spider moved closer.

If she'd been in any other situation, she'd be out of that bed and outside. Clenching her body, she pressed her lips together. Run. Hide. What should she do? Afraid to take her gaze off the hairy bug, she waited. It was almost to the blanket when pain shot through her leg and she squealed.

The cowboy had sat on her ankle. He jumped up, momentarily dancing on one foot.

BRUCE HAD FINISHED his shave and was going to change his socks and jeans. The second his butt hit the edge of the bed, something yelped then moved beneath him.

He leapt off the bed, pulling on his jeans as he rose. The blankets lay in a ball. Not the way he always left them.

How did an animal get in here?

"You little varmint, come out of there."

There was a rustling of covers before a woman jumped out at him. She took two steps and stood trembling in his arms. A fruity scent—strawberries?—wafted from the silky mass of blonde curls that tickled the underside of his chin. Her arms wrapped tight around his waist as she mumbled against his bare chest. Her womanly curves set off feelings he hadn't planned to have that morning.

Tingles ran up and down his entire body. His first reaction was to grab her and thrust her away. Instead, his hands clung to her as he listened to her smoky voice.

Through her gasps, he heard, "Spider! Bed! Bitten before!" She pointed back to the bed.

Longing welled up in him as he held her. "Lady, it's okay. It can't get you now."

She turned pleading blue eyes up to him. Her lovely features were shot through with fear. "Please, get it out."

With heart thumping and body on full alert, he slipped past her and lifted the blanket. A fair-sized spider sat on his pillow. The woman stepped back as he carried it outside on the pillow to release the ugly thing in the parking lot.

She'd given him a fright. His pulse still beat a rapid rhythm as he went back inside to find out what this female was doing in his trailer, and why the loss of her warmth against his chest when he'd released her felt bittersweet.

She huddled on the couch, holding the ripped portions of her blouse together. She'd been in some kind of tussle.

Wide, light-blue eyes locked with his, begging for something. Understanding, maybe?

Her fancy clothes were torn, dirty, and wrinkled. There was a bruise on her cheek and the beginning of a shiner around her left eye. Sympathy tugged at his emotions, but he stamped it down when he cleared his throat. Not the time to be soft. He was on a mission to pick up his boss's horses and had a schedule to keep.

"What are you doin' in here?" he demanded, regaining control.

"It was cold and I need a ride. My name's Amanda."

She wanted to make friends. Wheedle what she wanted out of him, no doubt. No way!

"I'm not takin' any passengers, lady." He pinned her with a no-nonsense stare.

She looked so pitiful he almost gave in to her plea. But Julia had taught him a hard lesson. Women were too much trouble.

They were in the middle of a forest with no town nearby. Leaving her on the side of the road was his first thought, but he didn't have the heart to dump her out and make her walk miles.

"Where are you goin', Amanda?" He pronounced her prissy name with disdain. No one he knew had that highfaluting name.

Her sad eyes brightened and, with a hint of a smile, she said, "Seattle," as if she knew the right answer.

Oh, good grief, that's where he was heading. What were the chances? He was all for helping people in need, but he'd looked forward to a week of alone time.

"You've got your nerve, gettin' into a man's trailer and hidin' out."

"I wasn't hiding. I fell asleep." She gave him doe eyes that were hard to resist.

"You can get a ride from someone else when we stop for breakfast. I'll take you with me to the next town." He reached into the cupboard and placed two cups on the counter. "Well, make us some coffee while I check the truck and turn on the generator." He shrugged into a heavy lumber jacket and shuffled out the door.

AMANDA DID AN inner happy dance as she searched the stranger's cupboards for coffee and filters. There had been some tense moments when she was certain he would make her get out. Something soft in the cowboy's eyes alerted her that he just couldn't bring himself to do it, though he clearly wanted to.

She found a new tin of coffee and made the brew the way she'd seen her maid, Sofia, make it at home. She figured out which was the 'on' button and pushed it. Proud of herself, she went into the bathroom to finger comb her hair and wash her hands and face.

She winced. There were bruises on her cheek and around her eye. A little makeup would help to hide the damage. If only she had some. A frisson of fear flashed through her as she remembered that horrible man's grubby hands on her.

She came out as the door opened and the cowboy stepped into the trailer. Grabbing her torn blouse, she pulled it together, hiding her lacy bra from his intense, blue-eyed gaze. The man exuded masculine prowess, sending a tingle straight down her spine. No one had affected her like that before.

She watched as his forearm muscles worked to remove a heavy blue shirt from the closet and toss it to her. "Here, wear this."

"Thanks." Grateful, she pulled it on over her blouse and buttoned the soft shirt. The hem hung almost to her knees. She poured him a cup of coffee, smiling as she handed it to him. Her hands trembled when she passed it into his callused grip. "What's your name?"

"Bruce. Bruce Palmer." His rich male voice resonated in the small space. He took a big mouthful, choked, and spat it out, narrowly missing her expensive Italian sandals. "That's dishwater. Are you tryin' to kill me?" While choking, he threw the rest down the sink and pinned her with a disgusted look.

Embarrassed, she tried to explain. "I don't make coffee at home."

"Well, I'll make a decent pot," he said, wiping at the dribble on his chin. He elbowed her out of the way, tossed the whole pot in the sink, and made a fresh one.

She drummed her fingers as she sat on the sofa watching his every move. What was he in such a twist about? At least she'd tried to please him. At home, one of the maids, Consuela or Sofia, always made it for her.

When the new coffee was ready, he handed her a cup, and she rested while he leaned back against the counter, taking large swallows. It wasn't the mocha latte she was used to.

"Do you have any cream?"

"There's two-percent milk in the fridge." The cowboy gave a disgusted snort.

She got up and poured a ton of milk into her coffee.

"What happened to your face and shirt?"

"I'd rather not talk about it."

"Hmm." He smirked. "You married?"

Surprised, her gaze flew to his. "No," she answered, her voice sounding defensive.

"Well, I don't want no crazed husband comin' after me 'cause I gave you a ride."

"Don't worry," she muttered. *My husband's dead*, she thought. The dreaded sorrow washed over her in a wave. Tears burned the back of her throat.

Bruce finished his drink and left his cup in the sink. "Well, Mandy, let's get goin'. We can find breakfast down the road. This here is a trailer and it's illegal to ride back here. You have to ride up front with me. So, come on."

"My name is Amanda, Amanda Vanderbilt," she said as the door shut behind him.

She took one last sip of the too-strong coffee and left the half-full cup on the counter.

The ride with this man was going to be difficult. He didn't like her, but she'd try hard to convince him to take her with him. She had too much to lose if he didn't.

CHAPTER THREE

AMANDA GLANCED SIDEWAYS at the handsome cowboy driving the truck. She'd tried several times to engage him in conversation, but he didn't respond. She'd never met any man who wasn't interested in her. Not that she expected the attention. That's just the way it always was. A man resisting her was new.

Her gaze rested on his flawless profile—a chiseled chin with the hint of a cleft in it, a perfectly shaped nose, and haunting blue eyes with long lashes. His old-fashioned sideburns curled slightly and needed a trim. A smattering of chest hair peeked out of his shirt where he'd left the top button undone. The view of it sent tingles right to her core.

His male scent and presence drew her as if she'd been magnetized. Irresistible.

Why was she so drawn to this ranch hand who couldn't possibly be her type? She'd grown up with the Kennedy and Aster children, along with her Vanderbilt cousins.

She crossed her arms, determined to put this foolishness over a cowboy out of her mind. Her whole life would change if she fell for someone like him, and she wasn't about to let that happen. And she wasn't about to have an affair with him 'for the fun of it,' as her girlfriends sometimes said. She definitely wasn't into that game.

The stranger had his radio set on a country station. The moment it came on, she wanted to cover her ears. She liked classical music. That's what she listened to and played at home. She'd taken lessons on her mother's grand piano since she was six. She wanted to hear *Fur Elise* rather than this jarring done-somebody-wrong song.

Without thinking, she grabbed the dial on the radio and spun it until classical music sweetened the air.

"What are you doin', lady? I liked that song." Bruce's gaze pinned her as he twirled the dial back to its original setting.

She clenched her teeth and glared back at him. "That song is horrible."

"No, it's not." He batted her hand aside when she reached to change it back. A classic battle of wills. She let him win.

For now.

Normally, people gave in to her. What was wrong with this man? Her arms crossed her chest, and her jaw became sore from clenching her teeth. She stared through the windshield, willing herself to block out the sound of his music.

Thoughts of Monica, her precious angel, had tears gathering in her eyes. Her anger slipped away as she thought of her sweet baby. Hopefully, she was still safe with Barb. Nothing on earth mattered more than her toddler and keeping her safe from the attacker. She'd be beyond lost if she lost Brad *and* Monica.

"So, lady, what's your story?" Blue eyes locked on her.

"What do you mean?"

"Why is your top ripped and your shoe broken?"

Noticing where his gaze had settled, Amanda pulled the shirt he'd given her together tighter and buttoned another button. What should she tell him? She wasn't sure what the man in the mask wanted. Was he after her, specifically, or just any woman who'd happened to venture into the garden?

Maybe she was being foolish. Perhaps he had no way of finding her. But could she take that chance? He'd said he'd find her, that she couldn't hide, and he'd said he knew where she lived, so she must still be in danger.

The cowboy cleared his throat as he waited for an answer.

"A man at a party became too amorous."

"Amorous? You mean familiar?"

"Yes." She rolled her eyes.

"Didn't your boyfriend step in?" He turned down the music.

"I don't have one."

"Well, your date then."

"No. I was there on my own. My friend Karin invited me."

"Where I come from, some man would step up and whup the guy that disrespected a lady."

Amanda's cheeks warmed, impressed with his chivalrous comment.

"I was alone when it happened," she mumbled.

"Even so, someone should give the dude a lesson in manners."

A vision of the masked face flashed before her. She'd only seen his eyes, light brown with colored specs in the iris. Beady eyes set close together. Black brows almost grown together in the middle. She shuddered and her nails bit into her palms.

The cowboy's warm hand tapped her cold ones. "Cheer up, Buttercup. He can't get you here."

She sure hoped he was right.

HUNGRY, EYES BLURRY from concentrating on the road, Bruce geared the truck down to pull into a truck stop. A huge, faded sign promising a home-cooked meal had his stomach growling.

His passenger was going to attract a lot of attention with a man's shirt over her fancy yellow skirt and a broken shoe, but there was nothing he could do about that. Her sun-kissed looks and cascading blonde curls were attention getters, too.

He pulled into the first available spot and turned off the truck. With his metal to-go cup in hand, he got out and spilled the cold contents on the ground. He trotted to the passenger door and opened it for her. Fearful eyes met his as he reached out to help her down.

"Don't worry, Buttercup. I won't abandon you to just anybody." She gave him a sheepish grin.

When she took her first few steps, she staggered on the broken heel. Grabbing her arm, he helped her negotiate the gravel parking lot. That heel had to go. He made her stop and hand him her good shoe. She held his elbow as she balanced on the broken sandal. He broke the heel off the good shoe and handed it back to her.

"What did you do?" her outraged voice protested. "That shoe is worth over three hundred dollars. The pair cost almost seven hundred," she informed him.

"Well, if ya can't walk on them, they're not worth much. At least now you can walk on them."

Her mouth cinched into a tight round ball, Amanda shrugged off his elbow and headed to the door without him. Perhaps she was a woman's libber, or maybe he really had made her that angry.

He caught up to her at the door. "Mandy, it will go better if we act like a couple when we get inside."

"My name is Amanda." Her eyes widened as she peered up at him. She crossed her arms again. "I need to make a phone call and buy a disposable phone."

He waited while she made the purchase next door.

"Stick close to me and we should be fine," he whispered as he held the door open for her.

Just as he suspected, the men in the café turned to ogle her before they found an empty booth and slid in. The place had a red-and-white, retro-fifties look. Five truckers and a biker filled the counter stools. Any one of them could cause trouble. He'd seen it happen before.

He grabbed menus from behind the napkin dispenser and handed her one, hoping she'd concentrate on it instead of looking around. Bruce gave the men a hard 'back-off' look.

To keep her attention off them, he said, "What'll ya have, Buttercup?"

Her jaw clenched as she scanned the well-fingered, coffee-stained menu. She obviously didn't like the handle he'd given her, but the outfit she'd had on when he'd first got a good look at her was the exact color of the buttercups in the pastures where he spent his days. The prettiest yellow flower God ever made, in his opinion.

Her hesitation drove him to make a suggestion. "How about bacon and eggs? We'll fill you up before I leave you."

She pinned him with a doe-in-the-headlights glance. He was sorry, but he had no intention of giving up his private time to a passenger who was needy and probably being stalked by some crazed boyfriend or husband.

The waitress came to take their orders. Amanda hesitated over her order, so he spoke up. "I'll have three eggs over easy, crispy bacon, and brown toast."

The young woman checked him out while she wrote his order then filled his cup with coffee. The smile she gave him as she looked up several times said she thought he was darn fine.

He wasn't one to flirt, so he studied Amanda while she ordered.

"I'll have eggs Benedict with extra hollandaise sauce and toasted rye bread."

Was she kidding? What kind of place did she think she was in?

The server's mouth dropped open. "Lady, I don't think the cook has ever heard of that, let alone cooked it before."

Amanda's cheeks pinked as she mumbled, "French toast then, please."

The waitress rolled her eyes, snapped her order pad shut, and made a beeline for the kitchen.

"Mr. Palmer, I'd really appreciate if you took me to Seattle with you."

Did she just flutter her eyelashes at him?

"My name's Bruce," he mumbled. "And I have no intention of taking you all the way across the country with me."

Her generous lips formed the perfect pout. For a moment, he wondered what those luscious lips would taste like.

What was the matter with him? He gave himself a mental shake. Women were trouble with a capital T and he wasn't having any of it. When this meal was paid for, he was out of here, and Amanda Van…der…Built would be someone else's problem.

The waitress brought their meals. Bruce's stomach rumbled when he saw the fabulous food.

"Could I please have cinnamon?" Amanda asked the waitress.

Was she kidding? Syrup wasn't enough? That must be what rich people put on their French toast. He shook his head, poured ketchup on his plate, and took a big bite of his perfect eggs.

Bruce was still chewing when the roar of Harleys pulling into the parking lot stopped him cold. He stopped mid-chew and stared through the grimy window. A trio of weather-beaten bikes sputtered and went silent. Three mean-looking men in scruffy black leather and boots entered the café.

"Eat up your food," Bruce told Amanda in a whisper.

The truckers, he'd managed to stare down. Bikers, he wasn't so sure he could handle.

The restaurant had slowly filled with diners while they'd waited for their meal. The only vacant spot was a booth behind the one where they sat.

Amanda chose that moment to rise. "Excuse me, I'll just be a moment."

In her crazy getup, she was going to have to pass the men on her way to the washroom.

Oh, boy, here we go.

Bruce's breath stuck in his throat as she passed the first two bikers. Now, if she could just get by the one with all the chains. She was almost past the third one when he grabbed her hand.

"Get your hands off me," Amanda screeched in a hoity-toity voice.

This wasn't going to be pretty.

Bruce dug in his pocket, threw some bills on the table for their half-eaten breakfast, and stood up.

The biker's eyes turned stone cold. "What's the problem, little lady? Don't you want to have some fun?" His words slurred and his eyes didn't focus. He was drunk.

The truckers at the counter had turned back to their coffees. They weren't going to be any help.

Bruce faced the steel-gray eyes and said, "Sorry, my sister is from out of state."

Like that made any sense.

He grabbed Amanda's hand, wrestling it away from the man's meaty grip. She stumbled and hobbled on her heelless sandal as he dragged her out to his truck.

"What did you do that for? I need the ladies' room. And I really need to use the phone."

Oh yeah, the phone. They'd left it behind.

"Never mind. Get in," he ground out.

He held the passenger door open. The urge to put his hands on her butt and shove her in was overwhelming.

The café door banged. The men in the black leather sauntered out. She turned, squealed, and jumped in the truck.

Bruce slammed the truck door and fumbled for the keys in his jeans as he ran around the front bumper. The engine roared to life, and he spun gravel when he put the pedal down hard.

"Gee, lady, what were you thinkin' back there?"

"What?" She met his gaze with her innocent doe eyes.

"Look at the way you're dressed…how gussied up you are. Ain't but two things those bikers are lookin' for, and one is trouble. The other, well, you got that, too."

Amanda's gaze dropped to the soft blue shirt which didn't quite hide her cleavage. She gasped as if she hadn't noticed that the top few buttons had come undone. Realization and fear dawned in her expression.

"See my point?" Bruce muttered as he checked the rear-view mirror for the tenth time. He sighed his relief. Then anger took over. He had just spent his boss's limited money and paid for this crazy woman's meal, and he was still hungry. Left his to-go cup behind, too. Plus he was saddled with this highfalutin' gal who was walking, talking trouble. The only woman he had ever known that wasn't trouble was his mama. Then it came to him. Prettier the package, the more trouble inside.

I gotta' get rid of her, pretty or not…and soon.

CHAPTER FOUR

AMANDA HUFFED HER annoyance as Bruce charged down the black top. She'd only had a few bites of her breakfast and she still needed the ladies' room. Bruce had pulled her out of the biker's grip. Thank goodness. But did he have to be so rough? By the look of the biker and the smell of his alcohol breath, maybe he did.

"In the next town, we'll get you some better clothes," Bruce ground out.

"Good." She could sure use something better than what she had on. She hoped he had credit cards.

First thing she'd do, before going shopping, was call Barb and make certain Monica was safe. Pain stabbed her when she remembered her baby was alone with someone she didn't know well. The phone was on the seat beside her in the café. Gone.

Tears gathered in her eyes. Was she missing her mommy?

She batted at a rogue tear that slipped down her cheek. If only Brad was still alive, he would make sure no harm came to their daughter. Monica had been the center of his universe. He'd played with her every spare moment he'd had, showing her how to rock her baby doll and stack blocks.

Crushing grief stopped her breath for a moment. Overcome, she hung her head.

"You okay, Buttercup?" Bruce's deep voice held concern. When their gazes connected, his eyes were soft and warm.

He really did care how she felt.

"I'm just thinking about a family member," she told him. Amanda wasn't ready to share the heartache of losing her husband. She didn't know how Bruce would feel about the way Brad had died—something akin to a mob hit with one bullet to the back of the head. The police wondered if he'd been involved in something sinister. The man she'd loved so dearly wouldn't be mixed up in anything illegal. They were wrong. But still, suspicion hung over the incident.

As they traveled in silence for an hour or two, Amanda plotted ways to stay with Bruce, because being left on the street was not an option and she was comfortable with him. He didn't seem the type to be taken in by a sob story. The direct approach was probably best. If she had her credit cards, she'd offer money. But he didn't strike her as someone who needed a lot in his life. She saw he wasn't into designer clothes—worn blue jeans and a western shirt, sleeves rolled to the elbows, seemed to be his style.

He pulled off the highway and stopped in a town boasting two thousand people. The sign was faded, the first word illegible. Something Springs was the name.

Bruce talked to another customer while he pumped gas. Amanda used the public washroom and quickly got back into the truck before he could pull away without her. Thank goodness, he hadn't. Her diamond-studded clutch was on the front seat. She'd have really been out of luck if he had taken off with it.

Bruce paid for the fuel and jumped into the driver's seat beside her. "They have one store in town that sells clothes. We'll head there now."

"Good." In a town this small, there probably wasn't a boutique, but she hoped their outfits at the very least came from New York.

At the far end of the main street, Bruce pulled next to a long, low cinder-block building. Amanda's eyes widened as she took in the sign. Thrift Store.

"Oh, my," escaped before she had a chance to politely hold it back.

Bruce opened the truck door for her. "Come on, Mandy. Let's get you suited up." He held out his hand, waiting to help her step out. He must be delusional, bringing her here. Before she knew it, he'd pulled her out of the truck and, with a hand on her back, guided her to the door.

"I can't shop here," she whispered.

"We don't have a choice. This is the only clothing store for miles." He opened the door and tugged her inside. A faint musty smell assailed her.

She'd never been in a place like this. Her friends would die before they'd buy in a thrift store.

"Come on, Buttercup. We don't have all day." He steered her to a rack of sweaters. A yellow one, the color of her skirt, caught his eye. "Here, will this fit?" She pulled at the tag. *Yes, it would, but another person had worn it. Eww!*

When she nodded, he pulled her to a display of jeans. She found her size. There wasn't a designer label in the whole pile.

"Do you need to try them on?" Bruce asked in a helpful tone.

"I can't wear these clothes."

"Why not?"

"Someone else has had them on," she whispered.

Surprise lit his eyes. "That won't hurt you," he said as he grabbed more items and marched her to the cash register. It was a metal box on a table.

A red-haired woman in a dark navy uniform, with S's on her lapel and tiny stars on the epaulets, served them.

Bruce laid a cream-colored cardigan and a second pair of jeans with the outfit they'd picked out. He'd snatched them off tables as they passed. A long white cotton nightgown had caught his eye and he'd added it.

The lady asked a ridiculously low price for the clothes. Amanda was so reluctant to pay for them, Bruce had to help her open her clutch and hand the woman cash. With the purchases bagged, they walked back to the truck.

When Bruce plopped the bag on her lap after getting into the truck, she tried to explain again. "I can't wear these."

"What's wrong? The outfit you have on is causing problems. You need something else to wear."

"Someone wore these."

He stared, annoyance and disbelief plain in his expression. "All right. If we wash them, will you wear them?"

She hesitated then nodded.

"Okay, we passed a Laundromat about halfway down the block."

BRUCE HAD PLANNED to do laundry, but not this soon. This woman began to make him wish he'd tossed her out. After he got her sorted, he'd be on his way and make up the time he'd lost.

When they left the truck to go in, she said, "I need all of the clothes I have on washed, too."

It took him a minute, but then his cheeks heated as he realized she wanted her underwear washed.

Oh, anything to satisfy her and be rid of her. "Okay, go to the trailer and hand them out to me. Hurry. I'm way behind schedule."

It wasn't long before a shapely arm handed out a bundle of wrapped clothes. She obviously didn't want him seeing her undies. Well, he was going to have to touch them when he washed them.

It wasn't as if he hadn't seen a woman's underwear before. In his wild and crazy days—his late teens and early twenties—he had drifted away from his Christian roots. Sown his wild oats, as Kohkom called it.

As the washer sloshed, he sat alone, remembering how his life had changed when he got word that his brother, Matt, had cancer. Bruce's stomach clenched as he relived the horror of the news. He was two years younger, but they had been inseparable growing up. They'd defended each other from bullies, and rode double on the one bike they had. Bruce smiled and thought of the many times he'd taken the blame for things his wild sibling had done.

Kohkom, their Cree grandmother at Indian Head, Saskatchewan, had raised them after their parents died when their snowmobile went through the ice on a lake in the Qu'appelle Valley.

Matt's diagnosis had brought Bruce up short and forced him to reconsider the way he lived his life. He came back to a relationship with God. He'd stopped running around, drinking, and sleeping with women. He'd determined to get close to his Maker once again and live a life honoring Him.

His chest swelled. He was proud of the decision he'd made. He looked forward to seeing Kohkom, as she was called in Cree, and Matt, when he swung north into Canada during this trip.

WITH AMANDA'S CLOTHES neatly folded and stacked in his arms, he tapped lightly on the door of the trailer, then opened it and stepped inside. Amanda lay asleep in his bed. The sight of her bare legs, peeking out from under the blanket she had wrapped herself in, made him gasp. Slender, muscled calves and pure-white skin held his attention. The wind caught the door behind him and it banged shut.

"Laundry's done, Buttercup." He placed the stack of clothes on the end of the bed. His breath hiked as her angel's face came awake. Long, silky lashes fluttered and opened to reveal dark, sleepy eyes.

Wow.

A pang of longing swept through him. How wonderful it would be to wake up to that lovely sight every day. Bruce swallowed hard.

"Get dressed, Mandy," he choked out. "I'll be back in five minutes."

Before he shut the door, a mess on the floor and counter caught his attention. That woman had left a cup on the counter when they drove away, and now there was a huge puddle of coffee to clean up. He found a rag under the sink, mopped the floor, picked up the cup, and then he left.

The quicker he got rid of her, the better.

AMANDA QUICKLY PUT on her 'new' clothes, not wanting Bruce to catch her half-dressed when he came back. Knots tightened her stomach as she planned how she would convince him to take her with him to Seattle.

There was time to mull over her situation. Sure, she'd never seen the man in the mask before. The strange, beady eyes and overgrown eyebrows deepened the mystery. Who could he possibly be? And why had he threatened to find her?

If she convinced Bruce to let her tag along, she'd have to share her problem with him. By staying, she might put him in danger.

Oh, goodness, she hadn't thought of that. He was strong and smart, capable of protecting her, but was it fair to do that to him?

Two thuds sounded on the door and he yelled, "I'm coming in, Mandy."

No time to think about her situation now, she decided as Bruce stepped inside.

"Well, I have to get going, Buttercup, so where do you want me to drop you? A guy says a bus comes by on the highway weekdays at noon. Or you can call someone to come get you."

Butterflies fluttered in her stomach as she launched into her plea. "I wondered if you could possibly take me with you to the next large city. I'd have a far better chance of getting a ride there."

Indecision knit his brow. She waited, hoping he'd take pity on her. She needed this man's protection, and she was afraid to be alone here.

She squeezed her hands into fists as she waited.

CHAPTER FIVE

GRIFFIN PULLED HIS gray hoodie over his head. He rubbed at his bone-cold left arm, damaged years ago by his brother when Griffin hadn't done his bidding quickly enough. His pulse sped when he glanced at the GPS monitor.

Cackling with glee, he rolled down his window and spit. The blip on the screen, his prey, was almost within reach. The tracker his brother had slipped into her purse at the party worked. It wouldn't be long now.

He changed gears the way his uncle had taught him, and the big rig climbed the incline.

Revenge was going to be sweet.

CHAPTER SIX

Bruce hated being in this position. It'd be cruel to leave Amanda stranded. He doubted she'd be able to fend for herself.

She looked alluring in the yellow sweater he'd picked out. It showed off her curves to perfection. She had more than enough to make a man's eyes linger.

Was that why he wanted to give in?

"Okay, but only to the next city."

He would likely regret this, but he didn't have the heart to cast her out.

The crazy woman jumped up off the couch and threw her arms around his neck.

Shocks of heat blasted through him as her feminine curves molded to his torso. For one brief second, he allowed himself the pleasure of hugging her back and drowned himself in the essence that was Amanda. Breathing deeply, he rode a wave of ecstasy.

What was he doing?

Flustered and annoyed with himself, he blustered, "Get off me, woman." With his body missing her warmth and her scent, he stomped to the door. "We're leaving in five minutes."

Why did he have to be attracted to this lady? Way above him socially, she was far better educated, and she'd probably gone to university while he'd only graduated high school. And she wasn't just pretty, she was beautiful. When speaking to him, she had an inner light that shone from her eyes that seemed just for him.

Good grief, he told himself, *give your head a shake, cowboy*. These thoughts would get him into a whole world of hurt. He couldn't be smitten with her. He couldn't let that happen.

The truck door opened and Amanda bounced into the passenger seat, far too cheerful for his liking. He saw her point, though. She had won this battle. Chicago was the next big city.

He didn't want to get involved with her, and he didn't want to care, but he wasn't comfortable dropping her off in a huge city. All kinds of bad things might happen to her. Maybe he could find a church or a woman's shelter that would take her in and help her get to where she wanted to go.

She settled in, and after buckling her seat belt, she put her manicured hands with the fancy, sparkly, pink nail polish in her lap. Even her hands cried 'rich.'

Bruce dropped the truck into gear. As they bounced over potholes, he drove out to the highway then onto the interstate. He guessed they would reach Chicago in the early evening.

Time for some supper, then some shut-eye.

Rather than turn on the radio and upset her again, he decided to talk instead. "So, Mandy, what are you runnin' from?"

"My name is Amanda, not Mandy, and who said I was running? I just want to get out of town for a while."

"Something has you spooked. So you might as well tell me about it." When she didn't answer, he said, "I might be able to help."

Moisture gathered in her eyes, and he regretted what he had said, but he was willing to help. She seemed so vulnerable. He hated to see anyone cry and wished he could fix whatever bothered her. He patted the cold hands in her lap. "Come on, Buttercup. Tell me what has you so worried."

"I...there might be a man following me."

"What makes you think that?"

"While at a party, I went into the garden in the back yard, and a man in a mask grabbed me."

"Is that what you were trying to say before?"

She swiped at the moisture on her lashes. "Yes."

"You didn't say he had a mask on."

She gave a sheepish grin. "I didn't want to bother you with my troubles. I kneed him and got away. He told me he knew my name, and he'd find me because he knows where I live."

"Well, I don't think you have to worry now." His heart caught. Her expression had turned to one of fear. "I won't let anything bad happen to you."

Gee, why had he said that, especially now that he was going to drop her off in Chicago? Something could happen to her there. His feelings for her were getting complicated, and he didn't like it.

He would have to pray about it.

"Tell me something about you, Bruce." She obviously was trying to change the subject, and that was good, but he wasn't much for talking about himself. "Where are you going?" she prompted.

"I'm going to Seattle to pick up horses for my boss."

"Oh, so the trailer and truck aren't yours?"

"No, I'm just a ranch hand."

"What does a cowboy do all day?"

He pinned Amanda with a look. She had an expectant expression on her face, as if she really wanted to hear. Those eyes sparkled at him with an inner light. His breath hitched. He swallowed, trying to think of something interesting to say.

No one would call his job glamorous, but he decided to plunge in. "I take care of horses, mend fences, go for supplies, muck stalls, brand calves. Things like that."

"I love horses. I imagine you use a western saddle. I took lessons and ride English."

"It wouldn't take much to switch to western."

What did he say that for? Now he had visions of riding with her. What was happening to him? He needed to keep his distance.

AMANDA KEPT STEALING glances at Bruce. *There's just something about a man in a cowboy hat.* His was black with a slightly rolled brim. His chiseled features drew her too, lean and fit from the work on the ranch. She hadn't met anyone who compelled her as he did. His looks, his voice, his body, the way he treated her, and his overall spirit.

She couldn't remember any man who'd affected her so strongly. It scared her, because he was just a cowboy. Not someone she would ever date or fall in love with. A Vanderbilt would never go out or get involved with a stable boy.

What would happen to her when he left her in the city? She couldn't stay on the street or in a shelter. The thought made her shiver.

She wrapped her arms around herself and stared out the window, praying he would take pity on her. She couldn't even imagine what would happen if he didn't continue to help her. Why, some street bum might accost her, or someone could see her wallet and try to rob her. The clutch alone was worth a lot of money. Her mother, who could spend a thousand dollars and think nothing of it, had given it to her one Christmas.

CHAPTER SEVEN

AMANDA TREMBLED WITH fear as they approached the city lights. It was dusk and her stomach rumbled. Bruce had agreed they would eat supper together before he dropped her off somewhere. That argument had heated until she assured him she could pay for her own meal.

"I'm sorry, Mandy, but I've a strict budget from my boss for meals and gas."

"It's all right. I have enough. I really wish you would let me come with you."

"Let's stop arguing about it and go eat." He parked, opened her door, and escorted her into the restaurant he had chosen.

He ordered a full meal, including steak, baked potato, cauliflower au gratin, and French apple pie for dessert. She chose a chicken Caesar salad. Her meager funds weren't enough for a full meal. When the food came, he bowed his head.

"Thank you, Father, for what we are about to receive. May the Lord make us truly thankful. Amen."

A wave of guilt stabbed Amanda. She hadn't said grace at mealtime since she was a little girl. The last time she remembered was when she had spent summers at Grandma Higginbotham's cottage in the Poconos. Grams and Higgy, as her granddad liked to be called, always took time to ask God to bless their food.

Was the cowboy religious?

She wouldn't care if he was, but it made her curious. This man had many layers. Too bad he wasn't going to keep her with him so she could discover everything about him.

When they began eating, he held his knife differently than she did. And he didn't mind talking with his mouth full, although he was discreet about it. Rather than put her off, as it would have upset her family, she found it endearing. She had always wished she could be like that, unassuming and normal, like the families on TV. Why did her family have to be so straight-laced? So prim and proper?

Bruce cleaned his plate and Amanda stuffed herself, figuring it might be a long time before she ate again. They each paid for their own supper and walked to the truck after she used the payphone to call Barb, and Bruce called his boss to check in.

"Where do you want me to drop you?" Bruce asked in the slow drawl he used sometimes.

Amanda licked her dry lips and said, "Bruce, you're going to park somewhere in the trailer tonight. Can't I please stay with you? I'll take the couch, and I won't be any trouble."

She watched him hesitate, thinking it over. She hoped that was a good sign. She held her breath, waiting. Seconds ticked by and she wrapped her arms around her waist, a habit from childhood that she'd never been able to break. It usually happened when she was worried or feeling vulnerable, like now.

His hands tightened on the steering wheel and then released. "Okay," he said.

Her breath released with a whoosh and Bruce looked surprised.

"You really are scared, aren't you?"

"Not now." She smiled.

BRUCE KNEW KEEPING her with him wasn't a good idea, but he couldn't bring himself to leave her stranded. He would have to eventually, but what would it hurt if he waited one more night?

He found a good place to park and jumped out of the cab of the truck to help her alight. They walked together to the trailer. He reached out to put his hand on her waist then quickly pulled it back before making contact.

He made hot chocolate, and then sat on the couch while Amanda washed up and put on her pj's, the soft cotton nightgown they had purchased at the thrift store. He sipped at his chocolate and prayed. He would need strength tomorrow to let this woman go. She was really getting under his skin to his soft side.

The door to the bathroom opened and a vision in pure-white cotton stood in the doorway. She looked beautiful. Virginal.

Oh, he was in trouble. He wanted her, right here, right now. Thank goodness, he had promised God he would behave himself or this night could've turned out very steamy. As it was, he could see it'd be a long, wakeful night. How was he going to sleep with the thought of her lying in his bed?

He jumped up and handed her a mug of hot chocolate. Before he could do anything about it, she sat beside him on the sofa with her dainty feet in view. When her bare legs made him react, he knew he was in for a sleepless night.

"Thanks, Bruce. I really appreciate your kindness."

"No problem, Buttercup." Now why had he used an endearment? That would only lead to trouble. If he thought about Julia's treachery, he could keep this woman from getting to him.

She played with a strand of her curly, long blonde hair. This was torture. He needed to get her tucked up for the night quick before he lost his resolve.

"Okay, Mandy," he said, standing up to put his cup in the sink. "Off to dream land. Take the bunk, and I'll bed down on the sofa."

"I don't mind the sofa."

"Ahhh...I sleep in the buff. You don't want me parading past you."

Her cheeks turned a pleasant shade of pink. She handed him her cup and quickly disappeared behind the curtain. He listened to the rustling sounds as she settled into his bed for the night.

AMANDA AWOKE TO clattering in the kitchen area. Dread gnawed at her and she rubbed the worry from her chest. If only she could find a way to get Bruce to take her with him. Then she remembered how he'd said grace at supper. She hadn't prayed for so long, but it was worth a try.

Heavenly Father, help me today. You know how frightened I am. Please, keep me safe, and let me go with Bruce. I feel so safe with him. Amen.

The prayer might not work, but she felt better as she took her clothes to the bathroom to get dressed.

At least she didn't have to worry about the masked man here. He'd never find her in Chicago.

"Well, Buttercup, I've decided to buy your breakfast this morning."

"Like a dying man's last meal?" she quipped.

"Don't say that, Mandy. You'll be fine." He drove back to the restaurant where she made another quick phone call to Barb.

"Hi, peanut. How are you?"

"I'm okay, Mommy. But I was crying for you." Monica's little voice choked up on the last few words.

"I'm sorry, sweetie. Mommy can't come home yet. You try to be a good girl for Barb." Tears threatened to spill as Amanda fought for control.

"Okay, Mommy. I love you."

"I love you, too."

Barb took the phone. "Please, don't worry. She's fine. I'm enjoying having her with me. But you need to make other arrangements. I'm going away in two days."

With moisture spilling down her cheeks, Amanda said, "Thanks. I'll call again soon and let you know who will be picking her up."

She turned. Bruce stood behind her. When he noticed her tears, he wrapped her in his embrace and held her. Shocked and stiff at first, she let out a long sigh and then allowed herself to hug him back. It felt so good to be in a man's sheltering arms. Safe and protected. His brushed cotton shirt was soft against her cheek, and he smelled wonderfully male. His chin nuzzled her hair.

Intimacy must have been absent a long time for him, too.

He broke the spell as he thrust her away from him. He looked scared and confused as he gazed into her eyes. Did he feel something for her?

She waited for him to speak.

"Use the washroom. I'll wait in the truck."

"I need to call my mother, so I'll be a couple of minutes." She dialed her mom's cell phone and waited while it rang.

"Hello, Mother, this is Amanda. I need a favor. Can you pick Monica up and keep her for a few days?"

"Your dad and I are leaving for Europe tomorrow. I won't be able to."

"Gee, Mother, I'm really in a bind. I'm out of town and can't get back."

"Well. The only thing I can do is take Monica with me. Is that all right?"

Disappointment hit like a ton of bricks, but what else could she do? If her daughter was out of the country, she'd definitely be safe.

"Okay, Mom. Just not too many treats. And bedtime on schedule." She gave her mother Barb's address. Before they ended the call, her mom promised to call Barb and arrange for a time to pick up Monica.

Amanda took her time in the washroom, knowing that soon she'd be on her own. Never to see Bruce again. Emptiness settled in her midsection like a heavy rock. Depression washed over her as she dried her hands and threw the paper towel away.

She opened the bathroom door and stepped out into the hallway near the entrance. A lady with a toddler in tow pushed past her to go inside. A man stood using the ATM, facing her, his gaze intent on the machine.

The man had overgrown brows that met above his nose. Brown eyes with specs in the iris. That was all she'd been able to see through the slit of the ski mask that night when he'd chased after her under the streetlights. She looked again to be sure. Beady eyes set close together.

It was her attacker!

Her heart hammered against her ribs. A wave of heat hit her face and she thought she might pass out. Unsteady, she grabbed the nearby wall.

He hadn't noticed her yet. He concentrated on getting money from the restaurant's money machine. Her chest tightened and another wave of heat almost dropped her to her knees.

She sprinted to the entrance and ran full out to the truck. Bruce saw her, leaned over to the passenger door, and opened it for her.

Straightening, he asked, "What happened? What's wrong?"

Her words tumbled out in a garbled mess. "It's him. The man in the mask. He's here!"

Bruce's brows furrowed. "What are you talking about?"

"The man who attacked me. He's using the ATM. He found me." The last came out in a wail. "Bruce, it's him. He has eyebrows that meet in the middle and the color of his eyes is the same."

BRUCE STRUGGLED TO comprehend what Amanda had said. How could her attacker have found her? Was she trying to trick him? But, as he considered this, a man dressed in a gray hoodie fitting Amanda's description exited the restaurant.

"Go, go. Bruce, please, go."

Looking totally panicked, she glanced back and forth between him and the man who was now running toward the road.

He dropped the truck into gear and spun tires on the pavement to get away. Thank goodness, he had started the truck already. He saw the little creep running toward a semi parked along the edge of the lot.

Amanda sat beside him, wringing her hands, trying to get a view in the side mirror.

"Don't worry. I'll try to lose him."

Bruce heard the blood rushing in his ears as he passed cars and other vehicles, trying to make it to the freeway where he hoped he could outrun the big rig. The horse trailer had him worried. It would slow him down to the point where the other truck might catch him.

At the back of his mind, something didn't sit right. How had this guy found them?

Amanda was crying softly beside him. "Bruce, I'm so sorry I involved you in this."

"It's all right. We'll talk about it later." He patted the cold hands in her lap.

His heart broke for her. She looked so forlorn. He took a deep breath and determined that nothing would hurt her as long as she was with him. Something about her had him hooked, and he would walk through fire to protect her.

The big rig was about five vehicles behind. Bruce saw it in the left-side mirror. They approached a curve, which meant the semi couldn't pass the cars between them any time soon. Bruce's mind raced as he weighed his options. He didn't know the surroundings, so he couldn't take another route. If only he was on the Canadian side of the border. He knew the area there, where he'd been raised. He stood a better chance of losing the creep there. But they wouldn't even get to Winnipeg until tonight, and his brother's farm was still a long way off. Once the truck hooked up on the TransCanada Highway in Winnipeg, Manitoba, they could try to make it to Indian Head in Saskatchewan, where they'd be able to hide. The problem would be to keep Amanda safe until then.

He tried to read the name on the side of the semi, but it was impossible. The rig was so dirty some of the letters were illegible, and now he was too far back to decipher the rest.

"How did he find me?" Amanda turned to him with round eyes and a furrowed brow.

"I don't know. It doesn't make sense that he could find you out of the blue like this. What do you have with you that you took to the party?"

"Everything." She had that deer-in-the-headlights look again. Light dawned on her face. "My purse!" She scrambled around looking for it. She gasped. "It must be in the trailer. I thought it was too flashy with all the diamonds on it to take it into the restaurant."

Her blue eyes appeared pained and grave. "My clutch, that's it. When I was at the party, a tall, thin man knocked it out of my hand. He bent down and picked it up for me. When he handed it back, he had an odd smirk on his face. As if he knew something I didn't." She mulled that over for a minute.

"Could he have put a GPS device in it?" Bruce searched her face.

"Gee, I don't know. Wouldn't I have seen it when I got money out?" she wondered aloud.

"How many compartments are there?"

Again, her face lit up. "There's a zipper on the back to put car keys or a phone in. I haven't opened it."

"Well, we need to get far enough away from him to stop and check if he slipped a gadget in that pocket."

Tears gathered in her eyes again. "Bruce, I'm so sorry. I had no idea I would be putting you in the middle of this."

"It's okay, Buttercup, I need some excitement in my life." He didn't mean it, but he could see his answer put her at ease.

He checked the mirror again. The semi had moved up two cars. "The interstate is not too far. I'm going to try to outrun him. Then we'll duck in somewhere and get rid of the transmitter so he can't find us."

Amanda heaved a big sigh and hugged herself.

CHAPTER EIGHT

MOTHS SWIRLED THROUGH Amanda's stomach as the truck barreled onto the interstate. Thank goodness she hadn't left Bruce before the attacker caught up to her. She didn't want to think about what would have happened to her if Bruce had dropped her off at a shelter as he'd planned to do.

After wracking her brain, she still didn't know why the unknown man was chasing her.

"Bruce, I'm trying to figure out why this guy wants to find me. It might be anything. My late husband was a surgeon who was murdered under suspicious circumstances. Sometimes surgeries don't turn out the way relatives hope they will. They don't account for the risks."

"But why would the man blame you?"

"Yes, I guess you're right. I'm not responsible for an operation my husband preformed. That doesn't make sense."

"Did you do something at the party that would have upset someone?"

She shook her head. "No. I didn't say anything that would make someone angry with me. I only passed pleasantries with a couple of my relatives. This is so strange."

"Have you noticed anyone following you before? Could you have picked up a stalker?"

"No. I think I would have noticed."

When she looked over at him, Bruce was praying, eyes on the road, his lips moving. It shocked her how comforting that was. A man who would pray for her. The urge to cry swelled within her.

"Maybe he wants to kidnap me and hold me for ransom. My parents are leaving the country. The authorities couldn't even get ahold of them." She was scaring herself.

Out of her peripheral vision, she caught sight of something. She screamed. Almost beside them at this point, the semi approached, ready to pass. No wonder Bruce had prayed. He'd seen it in the mirror, but rather than frighten her, he'd tried to outrun the big rig. Her nails bit into her hands as she watched the truck overtake them. Would he ram them sideways off the highway?

She counted the seconds as the huge truck overtook them. She huffed out a breath when he raced by. What was he planning now by getting in front of them?

As they crossed into Minnesota, the dirty rig stayed ahead of them.

"What is that guy doing?" Bruce asked. "He seems to be playing cat and mouse with us. He passes a car then he slows and lets them pass, then he's back in front again. Is he crazy?"

The semi slowed down as if he wanted Bruce to pass. "I'm not trying to go by him. I'm going to pull in for fuel while he's ahead of us."

"Good. I hope he'll just keep going."

They pulled off the interstate. While the attendant pumped gas in the truck, they ran back to the trailer. Before taking a washroom break, Amanda retrieved her diamond-studded clutch purse. She opened the outer pocket and gave it to Bruce. When he turned it over, a small computer chip fell into his large hand.

"Is that a GPS?"

Bruce rolled it in his hand. "It must be some kind of positioning device. This is how he found you so far from New York."

"But why would he go to all this trouble? Is it because I'm a Vanderbilt?"

"You might be on to something. He may want to kidnap you for ransom." He tossed the device out the window.

A chill rippled down Amanda's spine. Her parents would pay, but kidnapers often killed people after they received the money. She couldn't let it happen. What would happen to Monica?

"You look pale. What's wrong?" Bruce asked.

"I'm thinking of my little girl growing up without a mother."

"You have a daughter?"

"Yes, that's who I've been calling. Her babysitter. She's never stayed with this sitter before. I've been worried. I hope she's safe there, because no one, not even my mom, would look for her there. My mom has promised to pick her up and take her away with her to Europe."

The attendant walked up to the window and Bruce paid for the gas. The man had gone into the station to get change when the sound of a diesel engine gearing down made them both look toward the noise.

The big rig roared, sending waves of panic through Amanda's whole body.

The man with the bushy eyebrows drove into the parking lot, head bobbing as he grinned. He pulled up beside them. Bruce turned the key in the ignition and tramped on the gas. Tires squealed as the pickup and horse trailer shot across the lot to the highway.

"Is he coming?" Bruce asked.

Her throat had jammed, making it difficult to answer. She swallowed twice. "Yes, he's pulled back onto the highway. Bruce, I'm so scared. What are we going to do?"

"Whatever we have to, to get rid of this creep," he barked.

Amanda's heart pounded against her ribs, making it difficult to breathe. She scrunched down in her seat and watched the semi in the mirror beside her. The thing was ugly. Dirty as if never washed. Bugs and bug guts covered the front grill. The sight made her gag. There was a sticker visible on the bumper, but so filthy there was no way to read it.

She watched in horror as he gained on them. "He's coming," she screamed.

She looked at Bruce. His face was set in determined concentration. Something rammed the trailer and their truck shuddered and veered into the wrong lane. A red SUV drove toward them. Amanda held her breath as Bruce growled his annoyance.

Bruce fought with the steering wheel and swung them back into the right side of the road as the SUV whizzed by, its horn blaring. "He's going to kill us," Bruce thundered.

Her sobs escaped. They couldn't be held back any longer. She scrunched down again to see where the huge truck had gone. He hung back, slowing the procession of cars behind him. She imagined him chortling with glee.

A nightmare. Worse than a nightmare. Her life had never been threatened before. How were they going to survive this?

She looked to Bruce for strength. He turned his dark blue gaze on her. He smiled a reassurance he probably wasn't feeling. He patted the hands in her lap. "It's okay, Buttercup." His words gave her all the fortitude she needed.

She grabbed his hand and squeezed it to let him know she appreciated his support. When he'd called her Buttercup, his voice softened with fondness.

"Thanks, cowboy," she murmured, holding back more sobs that threatened to spill out.

BRUCE RACED BACK to the interstate. The truck flew down the highway at breakneck speed. He wished he could find a cop now. But, of course, when needed they were nowhere to be found. His breath came in gasps as adrenaline coursed through his body. He had no time to ponder how or why he got himself into this mess. Too late for that. All he knew was he had to make it to his brother's where they'd hide and she'd be safe.

He wouldn't let anything happen to Amanda. She was precious. Strange…a few hours ago, he was desperate to get rid of her. Now he was willing to risk his own safety to ensure hers.

In his side mirror, he caught sight of the big rig about a hundred feet behind them. He seemed to be coasting along, waiting for his chance to taunt them again.

Bruce looked over at the beautiful woman beside him and prayed nothing bad would happen to her. Far above him socially, she would never be his, but she was worth every gamble he took to keep her safe. He wished for the chance to wipe the tears from her cheeks.

Bang!

He was harassing them again, slamming into the back of the boss's trailer this time. Bruce ground his teeth and gripped the steering wheel tighter. He had a mind to stop the truck and pound on this little creep. But, with his luck, the guy would run him over before he had a chance to face him.

The semi pulled up beside them. The creep waved and sped on by.

Now what? Did he plan to lie in wait up ahead? Maybe set a trap?

CHAPTER NINE

A COUPLE OF hours had passed when Amanda's sweet voice broke through his troubled thoughts. "Bruce, I need the washroom."

"Can you hold off for a while?" He scanned the road ahead.

"I've been waiting for some time."

"Okay, the next exit we'll pull off."

There was no sign of the big rig when Bruce found a gas station not far off the interstate. He pulled the truck up to the gas pumps. Amanda jumped out to use the washroom.

When she came out, there was still no sign of the creep. Was he waiting ahead?

Bruce leaned out the window. "We're okay for now. You have time to make a phone call…make sure your mom picked up your daughter. I'll keep the truck running."

She gave him a grateful smile and hurried back inside the station. When she returned, he asked, "Will you sit in the truck while I make a pit stop and buy some food?"

When she headed to the passenger side, he spoke again, "I need you in the driver's seat in case he comes back. We'll need a quick getaway."

"I don't drive standard shift every day," she said with an apologetic grimace as she passed the front grill.

"He probably won't be back." He stopped after stepping out of the cab of the truck. "Did you get a hold of your mother?"

"Yes, she picked up my daughter, so I don't have that worry anymore."

When he came out of the store with a bag of groceries, the whine of a diesel put him on full alert. He dashed to the passenger side and dove in. "Go! Go, Mandy," he shouted.

"I don't know how. My dad only showed me how to drive stick shift in the Porsche a couple of times. I forget. You have to remind me."

"Put both feet on the pedals. The two on the left. Now slide it into gear." He grabbed the shift and shoved it into the right position. "Okay, push down on the gas with your right foot and slowly lift your left off the clutch."

The truck and trailer made a huge leap forward and the tires spun.

Tension drained the color from Amanda's face. She steered onto the blacktop and sped toward the divided highway.

"I'm so scared I'm going to crash. Is he coming?"

"Yes, but he's way back and you're doing fine."

He helped her shift through the gears until she was running full out. Some of the color had returned to her face, but her hands shook on the wheel.

This was a bad situation. With an inexperienced driver pulling an extra-long trailer, a disaster could happen on the first sharp corner. He had to calm her down.

[57]

Her strangled voice asked, "How am I doing?"

"Good," he managed between tight lips. At least that was the truth so far. "Haven't you driven your daddy's sports car?"

"I drive my mother's SUV, and it isn't standard. It's automatic." She gave him a challenging glare.

Perhaps she wasn't brought up quite as ritzy as he'd thought. But still, she didn't deny that her father had an expensive sports car. The truck was a far cry from her parents' expensive cars, no surprise there. Bruce's dad had been lucky if he was allowed to drive his boss's beat up old farm truck once in a while. He'd worked as a ranch hand all his life and it was the only life Bruce knew, too. A natural progression after high school, he took a job doing what he loved best, breaking horses and taking care of cows.

He needed to stop daydreaming and watch the road for the Creep. Perhaps once they reached Winnipeg they'd lose him in the city streets.

"That food smells good. Please, pass me some?"

He rummaged in the bag at his feet and came up with a plastic-wrapped sandwich and a soft drink. He unwrapped the egg salad sandwich and popped the cap before handing her the soda. Her hands still trembled, but the Creep hadn't tried any funny stuff for a while, and she had calmed down a bit.

They drove on until the setting sun lit the western sky pink.

"I CAN'T DRIVE this thing in the city." Amanda's voice woke him.

"Sorry, I must have dozed off." He rubbed his knuckles at his eyes, trying to orient himself.

"It's all right, I did okay. Our friend disappeared for a long time. I think I see him about five cars back."

"We have to find somewhere to switch places. If possible, pull off at the next exit. I'll help you gauge your speed on the ramp."

"Good, I'll be glad to have you take over. Bruce, I'm very grateful for all you're doing for me."

"It's all right, Buttercup." He gave her what he hoped was an encouraging smile and a wink. "Hey, I just thought of something. If this guy doesn't have proper papers with him, like a passport, he won't be able to get into Canada."

Amanda's eyes grew large and round. "I don't have any papers. Not even a driver's license."

"Yipes. That's going to be a big problem when we hit the border." Bruce let out a long breath.

"Please, don't make me get out and leave me," Amanda pleaded.

"Buttercup, we're a team now. You'll have to hide in the trailer, though, and hope they don't inspect it."

He guessed if she was caught, he'd be arrested, too, but it was a risk he would take. She had wormed her way into his heart, and he couldn't imagine going on without her. He'd never see her again after this trip, but that didn't matter. He'd keep her with him as long as possible.

AT FARGO, THEY were far enough ahead of the Creep that Amanda was able to pull into town and find a quiet place to switch drivers. A huge weight off her shoulders, she settled comfortably into the passenger's seat. Bruce could have the stress of trying to outrun the semi. A gnawing sensation stayed in her stomach as they drove north past Grand Forks. Hopefully, when they drove into Canada, the tanker wouldn't be able to follow. She prayed while Bruce drove on, keeping the semi behind them.

When they neared the border, Bruce pulled off on an exit ramp, found a gas station, and settled her under the covers on the bunk. He fussed for a few minutes, putting his duffle bag and a box of food at the edge of the bed to hide the lump she made in the blankets.

"Wish us luck, Buttercup."

"I'm praying," she whispered.

The door clicked closed behind him and she was alone. The truck rumbled back onto the road, then onto the smoother pavement of the divided highway. Whatever was about to happen, her fate was in the hunky cowboy's hands. And God's, she guessed. No matter what happened at the border, it would be better than the Creep catching her.

She knew the minute they came to the Canadian border. The truck stopped and started several times as they moved up the line to the patrol gatehouse. Every time the truck moved again, she prayed they would keep going, but they chugged to a standstill again. Her nerves were taut as a string on a bow when she heard voices speaking in the distance.

That would be the officer asking Bruce questions. She clutched her knees tight to her chest as she lay on her side and tried to remember to breathe.

She waited for them. The trailer shuddered when someone stepped into the stalls at the back. The door squeaked as it slammed shut. Then they stepped into the RV part of the trailer, and she held her breath. This was the moment.

She heard Bruce explaining the papers he needed to purchase the horses in Seattle. "These are the papers I told you about. They're a purchase order for the quarter horses my boss, Hank Sheffield, is buying from Hickory Acres in Seattle, Washington."

"Why do you need to come into Canada then?" an older male voice asked.

"My brother is sick with cancer, and I have to see him before…you know."

"Well, okay. Be on your way. And good luck with your brother."

The floor rocked when the officer and Bruce stepped out. Amanda threw the covers off her head, rolled onto her back, and breathed a huge sigh. They would make it through.

I hope Bruce holds it together.

He was the one who had to look the man in the eye and pretend there was nothing amiss. The urge to open the curtain in the bunk and peek out was strong, but if she got the attention of the agent, they'd be caught. She wrung her hands instead.

The truck rolled forward and kept going. She did her version of a seated happy dance. Bruce drove for about five minutes, and then the truck pulled onto gravel at the side of the road.

She hopped out of the trailer and headed to the truck. Bruce met her at the front of the cab. He grabbed her up in his arms and swung her off her feet in a circle. She buried her face in his neck, and yelled, "Hurray."

"We did it, Buttercup," he purred in her ear. He set her down, both of them breathing hard and smiling.

"That should be the end of the Creep," Bruce said with confidence.

"I sure hope so."

"Come on, let's find somewhere to park for the night."

He held the truck door open for her. It gave her the feeling of being cared for and cherished. Her friends were all women libbers and thought men holding doors open for them was passé, but Amanda loved it.

They drove north into Canada then turned left on Highway One, the TransCanada.

"This highway stretches from east to west across all of Canada. We follow this and my brother is not far off this road at Indian

Head. He lives on a farm where we can hide out for a day or two and catch our breath. We need to go now in case the Creep was able to cross the border."

"I hope we lost him."

"Me, too, but he may be used to crossing into Canada in the semi, or at least have the papers he needs."

The elation she'd felt dropped like a rock to the bottom of her stomach. Maybe this wild ride was not over yet.

CHAPTER TEN

AMANDA WAS GRATEFUL when they found a campground near the highway. Bruce carried the bag of groceries he'd bought earlier into the RV part of the trailer. Amanda held the door open as he stepped inside.

"Can you make us a sandwich while I take a shower?"

"Ah...yes," Amanda said, hesitation in her voice.

Bruce found clean clothes in the built-in drawer and took them into the bathroom. The last time Amanda had made her own sandwich she was eight or ten. The maid and housekeeper had had the day off, her mom was sick in bed, and her dad had been away on a business trip. She didn't want Bruce to know her culinary expertise was as inept as her coffee-making skills, so she struggled to find what she needed to put a sandwich together.

She found lettuce and tomato in the small fridge along with butter and mayo. In another drawer, she discovered knives. She scolded herself for not knowing how thick to slice the tomato, or how much lettuce to put on the bread. She guessed at the mayo, too.

When it oozed out of the sandwich, she figured it was probably too much.

Bruce opened the bathroom door. Too late to worry about it now.

"I'll finish up making supper while you shower," he offered.

"Thanks." It would be good to get the day's grime off and shampoo her hair. When she stepped out fifteen minutes later, Bruce had made a salad and hot chocolate. They sat on the couch eating their meal. It was the second time Amanda hadn't dined at a table.

Nice, cozy, and comfortable. Her mother would not be pleased if she saw her now. This was not Vanderbilt etiquette.

Bruce ate his sandwich, his long legs stretched out in front of him. "Relax, Buttercup. We're in the clear now."

"Good. I'd hate to think this nightmare isn't over."

"Well, we're safe for tonight, for sure."

After making another cup of hot chocolate and passing it to her, Bruce asked, "What was your childhood like, Mandy?"

"A bit lonely. My mom always busy with charity events and my dad travelled a lot. My mother was particular about who I played with. It had to be one of her friend's children, not someone I met at the park while out with the nanny or at private school. She was afraid the other children's bad manners would rub off."

"That's pretty harsh." He bit into a plum tomato.

"I guess it was the way she was raised." Amanda dropped her gaze.

"I was brought up totally opposite. My brother and I grew up with the Cree kids at Indian Head. My Kohkom…um, grandmother, lives on a farm, the same one my brother lives on now. My mom's Cree and my dad's white. His people were from Great Britain, Scotland, I think."

"Other than your skin color, you don't appear Native American."

The edge of his lips lifted the tiniest degree. "Wait until you meet Kohkom, she's very old school. She knows some awesome legends and stories. I'll have to try and get her to tell some while we're there." He took her cup and put it in the sink. "I can't wait to see my brother and spend a day with him. Find out how his chemo is going. Man, if he has no hair, I'm really going to tease him. Get back at him for all the pranks he played on me over the years."

Amanda heard affection in his voice. He clearly loved his family. She looked forward to meeting these down-to-earth people who were so different from those in her world.

"Well, we need to get an early start in the morning. I'm going to fill the trailer's tank with more water and check the equipment before I turn in."

Amanda sang an old church chorus as she prepared for bed, something she hadn't done in years. She was tucked up in the bunk when Bruce came back.

"You have a beautiful voice. What's that song you're singing?" he asked as he clicked the door shut and locked it.

"It's one I learned in Sunday school when I was little. You must be having an influence on me, because I haven't sung it in years."

"You don't go to church, then?"

"Oh, yes, I attend services every Sunday. My family wouldn't think of not attending church."

"Would you like to pray together before we turn in?"

Immediately her cheeks heated. *Pray with another person? He must be kidding.*

He grabbed her hand and bowed his head. "Father, we ask You to keep us safe. Help us to use Your wisdom in the decisions we make. Keep us humble. In Jesus' name, we pray. Amen."

Bruce turned out the lights and settled himself on the couch.

Amanda lay in the bunk, wondering about this man. Did he really believe God would keep them safe? And what was that about using God's wisdom. Humble. No one she knew was humble, except perhaps this cowboy. He was strange and somehow intriguing—someone she hoped to get to know better.

She breathed a sigh of relief. There had been no sign of the Creep, as Bruce called him, so for one night at least, she'd sleep in peace. Or at least try.

BRUCE HAD A good night's sleep and woke rested. Eager to arrive at his family's farm, he had washed, shaved, and had bacon and eggs cooking when Amanda crawled out of the bunk. Her pure-white, long nightgown they'd bought at the thrift store had his full attention as she tiptoed to the bathroom to change. It made him want to hold her face, gaze deep into her pale blue eyes and kiss her until he got a response. Do things with her he'd promised God he wouldn't.

I promised, but Satan sure didn't care, because he's bringing temptation to me every time I turn around. Please, God, give me strength, I'm so weak.

Holding her would be dangerous. He didn't want to complicate his life by doing something stupid. Now that he'd become a dedicated Christian, one night stands and casual affairs were a thing of the past. He would drive himself crazy if he kept thinking about her perfect body or her beautiful features.

Amanda stepped out of the bathroom. Bruce loaded a plate with bacon, eggs, and toast. She took it and sat on the couch.

"Thanks," she said, giving him a warm smile that hit him right in the solar plexus.

He hurried through breakfast, hustled her out the door, and into the truck. Then he emptied the waste tank and made a beeline back to the TransCanada Highway. They drove at the speed limit while Amanda hummed along to a country station that Bruce liked. It seemed she was beginning to like his music. This wasn't the alone time he had been looking forward to, but it really wasn't so bad either.

Bruce spotted a mud-stained semi in the mirror. Annoyance hit him under his rib cage. His pulse thrummed in his ears in a reckless rhythm. His palms spread sweat on the steering wheel. One at a time, he wiped them on his jeans, trying not to alarm her.

Not sure yet if the tanker was Amanda's masked man, he had a bad feeling about the image in the left mirror. He had trouble deciding whether to tell her or not. If he was wrong, he would worry her for no reason. If correct, she had a right to know.

He looked over at her. She'd finally lost some of the tension lines in her face. Perhaps the Creep wouldn't challenge them again, and he'd take her to Indian Head without upsetting her. He glanced in the mirror and fear grabbed his breath. The truck had moved up, and it was him, Amanda's beady-eyed creep. And there was only one vehicle between them!

If he bashed into them again, there would be damage done to his boss's trailer. He'd have to try to outrun him.

No way to spare her, he grabbed her hand. "Mandy, he's back."

"What? How could he be back?" The expression on her face just about broke Bruce's heart. Real terror bloomed on her features.

"I don't know, but he is."

This little creep made him mad. He tromped on the gas and the speedometer climbed to ninety. Amanda had a death grip on the edge of her seat. He took a second to check behind him and, sure enough, the semi came up on his tail.

This is in Your hands now, Lord. Please, keep us safe.

Inches from Bruce's bumper, the Creep could easily jolt him off the road. Depending on how he hit the ditch, there was a good chance the truck would roll and wreck his boss's equipment or, worse, kill them.

There was no telling what the man would do if he caught them. Would he kill her right there? Would he abduct her? She didn't seem to have any idea what he intended. Or why he followed her.

The semi's horn blasted. Bruce almost lost control when the wheels caught in the sand. He was headed straight off the road.

Amanda screamed and grabbed his arm. He cupped her head and brought it against his shoulder.

"It's okay, Buttercup. I'm not about to let anything happen to you." His voice rang with bravery that he didn't feel as he struggled with the wheel and gained control. The truck tires finally struck pavement again.

His gut had become a tight, painful ball. He'd held his breath so long he had trouble breathing. Amanda cried against his arm. He had to take his hand away, because the road curved a hundred yards ahead. He stayed in front of the big rig, barely. If he slowed for this corner, the rig might hit him and send him spinning off the road.

He hunkered down in his seat, with both hands on the wheel at ten and two, like the driving manual advised, and steered. Amanda buried her face in the sleeve of his upper arm.

He prayed desperately as the tires of the trailer caught in the gravel. Afraid he'd leave the road, he tried to compensate. With the truck still on the highway, he made the corner. With a sigh of relief he said, "Hey, you can look now. We made it."

"I thought we were dead for sure." She wiped at the tears that streaked her cheeks. "I was so scared Monica would be without a mother. Thanks, Bruce."

"Don't thank me. Thank God. He is the only one who could have helped us get around that corner. I've never been so worried and terrified in my life."

Bruce watched in the mirror as the semi kicked up dust. For a moment, he thought he might go off the road. The big truck slowed down and gained the pavement again. As he geared up to overtake Bruce, a couple of trucks passed him and they had a buffer of cars between them again. Bruce drove on, just above the speed limit, and tried to keep the big rig behind them.

The main goal was to get to Matt's ranch where they could hide out for a day or two and catch their breath. He'd erase that worried expression from Amanda's face and maybe she'd find some peace. She could phone her daughter again and reassure herself that she was okay.

"How you doin', Buttercup?"

"I'm fine. A little shaken."

A brave woman, no doubt about that. She wasn't about to let on how terrified she'd been. He liked that—he liked that a lot. She'd need to be strong because, apparently, the Creep wasn't about to give up.

CHAPTER ELEVEN

AMANDA ATE AN apple and watched the big truck following them. Bruce kept several cars between them as he drove.

"I need to get enough distance ahead of the Creep so that when we get to Indian Head, we can slip off the highway unnoticed."

"Can we do that?"

"All I can do is try." He patted her shoulder. "I'll do my best."

What more could she ask? She'd never had a man who was willing to work with her and make so many sacrifices. If they had rolled back there when they were going fast, either one of them might be dead now. She choked on the tears that threatened, and leaned over and kissed his cheek. "Thanks, cowboy."

He batted her away. "Enough of that kissy stuff, Buttercup. I'm tryin' ta drive here," he said with a bashful smile.

She grinned. It wouldn't hurt him to know how much she appreciated him.

Amanda counted vehicles as they went by them. When they passed a couple of semis, she rejoiced to put some distance between them.

"He must be low on fuel. He's pulling off," said Bruce

"Really?"

"Yes, he just turned into the gas station that we passed by. Now is our chance to lose him." He smiled, giving her a big high five. "I know a grid road we can take that will get us off the highway. A mile or two off the TransCanada, we'll hook up to a parallel road and it'll take us to the farm. It will be a dusty drive because it won't be paved, but he definitely won't find us.

"Oh, Bruce, That's great. Let's do it."

It was a longer, slower route, but Amanda didn't mind. Her pulse had slowed to a normal pace. The creases in Bruce's forehead were gone, and his grip on the wheel had eased.

They pulled into a long driveway, and Bruce honked the horn until they reached the house. Amanda smiled, enjoying his enthusiasm.

The house was surrounded with planted trees and bushes. Several outbuildings and grain bins lined one side of the yard. The white, two-story house had a grassy yard, and when they pulled up beside it, Amanda noticed a well-tended vegetable garden in the back. Flowers ringed the house—pansies, roses, and lilies. A large porch with banisters painted white ran across the front.

Outside the sheltering trees, pens held a variety of cows and calves. Horses grazed in a cluster further over. Amanda was amazed at the organized yard and freshly painted house.

A short, stocky woman opened the side door and stood wiping her hands on a flowered apron. She had a broad face with high cheekbones. Years spent outdoors had etched many lines in her brow and the corners of her eyes. She smiled and held her arms open, waiting for Bruce to turn off the truck and run to her. She enfolded him in a welcoming hug. His tall frame bent low to kiss her cheek.

Amanda got out and hung back, not wishing to intrude on their tender moment.

Tears wet both of their cheeks as they drew apart, and Bruce took Amanda's hand and brought her forward. When she was on the top step, he introduced her. "Kohkom, this is my friend, Mandy. We're traveling together to Seattle." He gave a sheepish grin, obviously feeling guilty about all the times he had tried to get rid of her.

Amanda allowed herself to be pulled into a soft, loving bear hug. "Welcome to my home," Kohkom said. She ushered them into a tidy kitchen. Kohkom had been baking. Balls of batter were set out on sheets ready to be cooked.

"What are those, Kohkom? Are they my favorite corn balls?" Bruce asked with a twinkle in his eye.

"Everything I make is your favorite." Kohkom chuckled. "Tell Mandy what they are."

Bruce turned to Amanda with that twinkle in his eye. "These have ground dried corn and Saskatoon berries in them."

Amanda saw some had already been fried with lard in a large iron skillet.

Bruce reached for one and Kohkom slapped at his hand. "Let them cool, son."

"Where's Matt?" Bruce questioned in a hushed voice.

"He's with the horses." Bruce turned to go outside. "You will find him changed."

"How?" Bruce asked, a worried frown on his brow.

"You'll see."

Bruce grabbed Amanda's hand and dragged her out and across the yard to where the corrals were on the other side of the sheltering trees. He let go of her hand when his brother came into view.

"Matt," he yelled and climbed over the fence into the corral where Matt was lunging a spotted horse. The horse was tied to a lunge tether that Matt was holding. The horse ran around him in a circle. Amanda walked up to the rails to watch.

He dropped the lunge line and ran into Bruce's waiting arms. They shared a big hug with lots of backslapping.

His color wasn't good. His skin was a sickly beige-green. It made Amanda wonder if his liver had stopped functioning properly. It would be from the chemo. He obviously wasn't tolerating it well. Her eyes collected moisture as she thought of the effect this would have on Bruce.

The men talked in excited voices as she brushed at tears. Bruce didn't need to see how upset Matt's appearance had made her. She pasted on a smile and waited for an introduction.

Matt looked to be about three years older than Bruce with similar facial features. She saw at a glance that they were brothers. Both had the same muscular build. Both had the same endearing smile.

Bruce made the introductions. "Matt, I'd like you to meet Mandy."

Matt held out his hand. "Hi. It's nice to meet you. My wife, Nola, is at work in town. You'll meet her later."

A warm, callused hand gripped hers. He held her hand a little longer than normal, as if he had become dizzy.

"It's nice to meet you, too. You have a lovely property here."

"That's Kohkom's thing. She loves plants and flowers. If you want to get on her good side, ask her about them."

"Thanks, I will."

They left the corral area and walked to the house. The men had started without her, as if they had forgotten she existed. She smiled to herself. These two siblings truly loved each other.

They entered the kitchen to the aroma of meat cooking. It appeared Kohkom was planning a stew of some kind for supper—the type that would simmer all afternoon. They each took a mug of coffee and sat in the living room. Amanda sat on the sofa and Bruce came and sat next to her. Kohkom sat in a rocking recliner and Matt chose a nearby chair.

Amanda listened as the men talked ranching. Kohkom straightened them out whenever they argued over something that had happened in the past. Amanda would never have imagined that farming would be so interesting, but the more they talked, the more questions she had. Matt and Bruce were only too willing to answer and explain things to her.

"When I go to feed the cattle, you can come with me and see what we've been talking about," Matt told her.

Strange, but she was genuinely interested to see how it was done.

Bruce promised to let her ride western saddle while they were there, something she had never tried before. Vanderbilts only ever rode English saddle.

The way they were raised was very different, but she liked the down-to-earth atmosphere here on the farm, and the pace of life—far less stressful.

At five thirty, a dark SUV pulled into the yard and a young First Nation woman got out. She was dressed in a chocolate-colored business suit, her long black hair swept up in a clip. She carried a briefcase and a bag of groceries as she came up the steps to the back porch.

Bruce rushed to open the door. He kissed her cheek as she swished by him. After placing her parcels on the counter, she went back for a hug. As she chattered in Bruce's ear, he winked at Amanda over the woman's shoulder.

They parted and he said, "Nola, there's someone here I'd like you to meet. Amanda is travelling with me from New York."

Amanda liked the pretty woman instantly. She was warm and friendly, with a welcoming attitude.

"You're from the east coast. Do you like the prairies? A lot of people think they're too flat."

"I don't think they are too flat. It's soothing." Amanda knew Nola was referring to the very flat, wide-open spaces with almost no trees. Miles and miles of fields full of grain crops.

"Wow." Nola turned to Bruce. "Where did you find her? She's a keeper."

Bruce gave them both a sly grin. "I picked her up at a gas bar."

Nola laughed. She obviously didn't realize he wasn't kidding.

Kohkom spoke up from her position at the stove. "Would you men get out of my house while the girls set the table for me?"

Amanda tried not to let the women know how awkward she felt helping Nola. At home, one of the servants would set the dining room with fancy china and glassware. Kohkom had mismatched plates and glasses. The silverware was from several different sets as well. Nola didn't bother with coffee spoons or dessert forks.

An hour later, they all sat down to eat and Kohkom asked Matt to pray. After grace, Nola asked for their plates and served each person the yummy-smelling stew. The homemade concoction had potatoes, carrots, and onions, with large chunks of meat swimming in rich, thick gravy. Bruce looked at her several times as if to see if she liked it. She smiled back and continued eating.

Amanda listened to the conversation as Bruce caught up on the working and finances of the farm. She was fascinated as they talked about new inoculations for the calves, problems with weed infestations in the hay fields, and the horrible prices the cows were bringing in. Her family had none of these worries. Her dad was always going on about the stock market and green fees at the country club. Two completely different worlds.

AMANDA'S EYES GREW big when Matt started talking about stud fees for his bull, and Bruce thought he better change the subject.

"Kohkom, why is there no bannock with supper tonight?"

"Sorry, son. I'll make some for you tomorrow. Maybe your girl will help me."

Amanda blushed a pretty pink. "She's not my girl, Grandmother. She's a friend."

Amanda leaned forward. "I'd love to help you and see how bannock is made."

Bruce smiled at the friendly gesture and squeezed Amanda's hand under the table. She gripped his hand then pulled hers away. He wasn't sure what to make of that. He didn't want her mad at him. It had become important that she like him.

Nola collected the dinner plates and brought out pie and ice cream. Kohkom had made Bruce's favorite apple crumble. Kohkom called it French apple pie. Everyone laughed when Bruce went for seconds.

His cheeks heated as he dug into the second piece—his heart aglow with happiness and peace.

Nola and Matt stole adoring looks at each other. There was nothing as great as being home with family, and the love of a good woman. Bruce couldn't help glancing at Amanda. Longing swept him from head to toe.

He cleared his throat. "After dishes are done let's go for a short ride."

"Great idea, bro," Matt chimed in.

Bruce looked into Amanda's amazing eyes. "It'll give her a chance to try riding western saddle."

"Wow, you don't ride western?" Nola asked.

"I've ridden English all my life."

"You'll love western once you get used to it," Nola told her.

Bruce and Amanda strode out to the corral and saddled four horses. By the time they finished, Matt and Nola joined them. Bruce gave Amanda a leg up into the unfamiliar saddle.

He helped adjust the stirrups. "You okay, Buttercup?" She nodded as her cheeks pinked again. He liked her reaction.

She took to western saddle as if she'd been riding that style her whole life. She sat easy in the saddle and handled the skittish horse like a pro. A soft, warm emotion settled in his chest.

He marveled at how this woman affected him. Opposite in tastes and culture, there was something about her he couldn't quite resist. He knew he should. He was setting himself up for a huge heartbreak when they parted.

Hopefully, by then, the Creep would be long gone or behind bars, and she'd go back to her hoity-toity life. And he wouldn't miss her too much.

Bruce could tell Amanda loved riding across the prairie by the happy expression on her face. They stopped at a coulee where some tall trees had grown up around a pool of water. They allowed the horses to drink while they sat in their saddles and chatted.

Bruce kept casting glances at Matt. Worry nagged at his stomach. He wondered how long Matt had and if his doctors thought they could cure him. It was the elephant in the room as they tried to fill the conversation with mundane, everyday things.

When the horses were satisfied, Nola challenged them to a race back to the house. Matt and Nola took off at a gallop while Bruce and Amanda ambled their way back.

"Matt has me worried," Bruce said. "He doesn't look good."

"No, he doesn't. My husband was a doctor, Bruce. I spent a lot of time helping in his office while he saw patients, and he doesn't appear well to me, either."

"How long do you think he has?"

"I'm sorry, I have no idea."

"It brings life into perspective, doesn't it?"

"Yes. It certainly does."

"I wonder why God would put him through this."

"I don't know, Bruce." Pain clutched her ribs as she thought of Bruce suffering the loss of the brother he loved. It was good he was able to spend time with him, but she sensed it might be the last time. Her knowledge of God and His ways seemed so shallow compared to Bruce and his family's faith. She needed to understand Him better, so she could comfort this man.

They reached the corral as the sun set behind the western horizon. A beautiful display of pink and red tinted the clouds long after the sun was gone.

"Sunset is amazing here," Amanda said, her gaze on the horizon.

"Yes, in summer it's light until ten o'clock." He lifted his saddle off. "You haven't lived until you've witnessed the northern lights."

"I've heard of them, but what are they exactly?"

"They are usually green, swirling lights that almost fill the northern sky. Sometimes they can be red, too. But I've never seen that. Air currents move them and they look like they're dancing in the night sky."

"Are there Cree legends about them?"

"Yes, we call them *Cipayak*, and if we can catch Kohkom in the right mood, she'll tell you a story about them."

Amanda helped put the tack away in an old shed. She'd never found anything like this culture that interested her so much. She hoped Kohkom would share her native stories and experiences. She wished she could stay and really get to know Bruce's people.

Bruce hung the reins and other tack on pegs on the wall and mounted the saddles on wooden crates. There was no light in the shed, and the air was musty and smelled of mouse droppings. Amanda handed her saddle to him and stood waiting in the dark. A beam from the bulb in the yard cast a small shaft of light across the floor. When Bruce turned, their gazes met in the dim light.

Amanda's breath hitched as he stopped and scanned her face. He looked like he wanted to kiss her. In that moment, in the most unromantic setting, she wished he would. His full lips seemed to hover above hers in the dark. She stood on tiptoes to meet him halfway.

His lips were warm and moist as the kiss took her to another place. Somewhere where only they existed. His large, callused hands held her hips and brought her closer to him. She felt the strength in his biceps as her hands clung to his shirtsleeves. It was the sweetest kiss, but it was over far too soon.

She opened her eyes when his lips left hers, and she teetered when he let her go. After grabbing her elbows, he smiled and held her.

"W-we need to get back to the house," Bruce whispered and hurried out of the shed. She thought she heard him mutter, "Sorry," but her heart was pulsing in her ears, so she wasn't sure.

A little shaken, she walked back to the house beside Bruce. Did he mean to kiss her or did he regret it now? The kiss had ignited a fire inside her that would be hard to put out.

The temperature outside had dropped when the sun went down, but the house was warm when they entered the kitchen. Confused, Amanda wished for some alone time to think about what had happened in the tack room. But that was not to be, so she took the mug of hot chocolate Nola thrust into her hands and sat at the far end of the table, dazed.

Bruce was busy talking to Matt, so she couldn't catch his gaze to try to analyze what he was thinking or feeling. The unexpected kiss turned her emotions inside out. She had liked it far too much. After all, this man was not someone she'd ever contemplate a future with, and yet a simple kiss in a shed had her pulse racing and wishing for more of those sweet, gentle kisses.

Kohkom sat in the chair nearest hers and patted her hand. "You all right, child?"

The woman's kindness brought a burning sensation to the back of Amanda's throat. "I'm fine, thank you." She gave Bruce's grandmother a bright smile. "I can't wait until tomorrow when you show me how to make bannock. I enjoyed the corn balls."

"And I will enjoy showing you," she said in the slow, lazy way she had of speaking.

When the hot chocolate was finished, Bruce said, "Well, Mandy, we should let these people get their sleep. Good night, everyone." He took her cup from her and ushered her out to the RV.

He hadn't called her Buttercup. Did that mean he regretted the kiss?

Later, as she lay snuggled in the bunk, she wondered about it. Safe and secure, she said the prayers she'd been neglecting for years and settled in for a worry-free sleep.

CHAPTER TWELVE

THEY'D VANISHED!

Griffin let out a string of curse words as he raced down the highway, looking for the white truck and trailer. How could he have lost them? His brother, Harold, would be steaming if he discovered he had lost the little witch. He'd been good and mad when Griffin had phoned and told him the smart aleck cowboy had found the GPS device and thrown it away. He'd had to promise to keep them in sight so Harold wouldn't become enraged again.

Harold could be vicious if things didn't go his way. Griffin had scars to prove it. He scratched at the one on his throat. It hadn't completely healed yet.

He hated the permanent limp he had after Harold had pushed him out of the apple tree in Mrs. Sykes' yard when he was ten. He'd never wanted to steal apples again. He'd been in pain for days trying to hide it from Mom. When she'd sobered up enough to notice the way he walked and took him to the doctor, the leg had healed crooked, and she refused to pay to have it broken and reset properly.

He hated the unnatural bald spot on the back of his head. It had happened the day Harold lassoed him, tied him behind his bike, and dragged him down the pavement. Griffin hadn't even been old enough to go to school when that happened. It seemed the older Harold grew, the wilier and more vicious he became.

It was worth his life to go drinking with him. Griffin never knew when he would turn on him and he would end up with broken ribs or a new scar from a flying beer bottle.

He understood why his brother was so awful mean. No one could grow up in their house and turn out anything but angry and abusive. But Harold took it to extremes, and he didn't care who he rained his wrath out on. He had never done a thing to deserve the abuse Harold handed out.

Griffin shook his head, trying to rid himself of the memories, then decided to turn around and patrol the miles of highway where he'd lost his prey. If he were lucky, they would come back to it again and when they did, he'd be waiting for them. He hoped he could find them, otherwise he'd have to tell Harold he'd lost them. He rubbed at his arm where it still hurt from the last time Harold wasn't pleased.

CHAPTER THIRTEEN

BRUCE HAD ALREADY left the trailer when Amanda arose the next morning. She was still conflicted about the kiss. Maybe it meant something and maybe it didn't.

After showering, she went to the house to get some coffee. After spending time on the road with Bruce, she realized she needed to learn to do things for herself. She didn't need to depend on servants to wait on her and fulfill her every whim, and learning to make bannock with Kohkom was a beginning.

The aroma of bacon frying met her when she stepped into the kitchen. Nola handed her a plate of fluffy scrambled eggs, bacon, and multigrain bread. Bruce and Matt smiled when she took her seat at the table. It was odd that Kohkom wasn't bustling about the kitchen.

"Where's Kohkom?" she asked, hoping her question wasn't out of place.

"She's out back, building a fire," Bruce said between mouthfuls of egg.

"A fire? Like a campfire?" Amanda wondered why she would do that.

"She's getting ready to make bannock," Nola told her.

"Over an open fire?"

"Yep." Bruce sent her a saucy wink.

She felt her cheeks heat. Of course, Kohkom wanted to show her the way her people had been making bannock for years. It was a strange but cool idea at the same time.

"Should I go out and try to help?"

"No, wait until she comes in." Bruce shifted in his chair. "Kohkom figures everyone knows how to build a fire."

Amanda grimaced. She had no idea how to set the wood out to make a proper fire. In the movies, it looked like they made a miniature teepee with sticks of wood, but that was all she knew. How they got it to burn or stay lit was a mystery.

Kohkom shuffled through the door, her cheeks bright from the heat of the fire. Amanda helped clear the table and Nola did the dishes as Kohkom began the lesson. The boys cleared out, mumbling something about attending to the horses.

Bruce's grandmother mixed six cups of flour with a cup of lard in an old earthen bowl. She had Amanda stir in three tablespoons of baking powder and a tablespoon of salt.

"We usually put currants that we picked in here, but today we will use two cups of raisins."

Nola brought over three-and-a-half cups of water in a large pitcher.

"Pour it in slowly and work it up with your hands," Kohkom explained. When Amanda hesitated she said, "Come, child, get in there and mix it with your hands."

She didn't seem concerned about how clean Amanda's hands were, but she guessed that made sense if they were working outside near a campfire.

"Now you have to take it outside."

Amanda carried the large bowl and followed Kohkom to the fire. After the older woman divided the dough into quarters, she firmly wrapped the dough around one end of four sticks that were about four feet long, propping them securely over the fire. After about fifteen or twenty minutes, maybe longer, they turned golden-brown and it was time to take them off the fire.

"There's an easier way to do it," Nola whispered to Amanda. "You can spread the dough in a sixteen-inch square pan and bake it at four-hundred-twenty-five degrees for about twenty minutes. She's showing off because you're white."

Amanda chuckled as she carried two of the bannock sticks back into the kitchen. There was something cute and endearing about Bruce's grandmother.

Bruce, back from looking after the horses, took the sticks from Amanda and placed them on the counter. "How did you like making bannock?"

"It was all right. I can't wait for it to cool off so I can taste it."

"It'll be awhile. Do you want to go for a ride in the truck? I'll show you around the area." He had the sparkle in his eyes that she liked so much.

"Okay, let me go and change my top. I got some soot from the fire on this one." She brushed at a spot on the right arm of her blouse.

"Thanks for the lesson, Kohkom," she said as she left to go to the trailer. The day was bright and warm as she crossed the yard. Horses neighed in the corral and mourning doves cooed in the trees. Amanda took a large breath of the fresh air and sighed, contented.

BRUCE GAVE MATT a hug and left the kitchen to disconnect the truck from the trailer. Matt was going to lay down for a nap because, by midday, he was out of energy. Bruce worried about him, but there wasn't anything he could do about it. His brother was in the midst of chemo treatments and would be going back for more after he and Amanda left tomorrow. Matt had told him the last dose had knocked him down, and he was finding it more difficult each time he went for another treatment. More nausea and less energy. Bruce wished there was some way he could do the treatments for Matt. Spare him the grief and aggravation. But since that wasn't possible, he'd have to pray things would turn out all right.

It came down to either he trusted God or he didn't. He did trust Him—he was finding it hard, though.

He unhooked the trailer and started the truck when Amanda appeared in the buttercup-yellow sweater Bruce loved. The yellow of the sweater highlighted the blue of her eyes. It was enchanting.

She hadn't mentioned Monica today. It was the first time she hadn't in days. He knew her daughter was the most important person in her life.

She smiled brightly at him as she climbed into the cab of the truck beside him.

He took her on a tour of downtown Indian Head first. It was nothing like the city she was used to, but she seemed to appreciate its quaintness.

"I'd like you to come to church with me tomorrow," he said as they passed the white clapboard building that needed a coat of paint.

She looked over at him for a long moment then said, "Yes, of course."

He wondered if her hesitation was because of the building, the denomination of the congregation, or something else. It really didn't matter as long as she was willing to come and hear the gospel preached.

When he took her out to show her the wheat fields, she voiced her amazement at the wide-open spaces and the fact there were very few trees.

"Oh, look, Bruce, a deer."

He chuckled and said, "We have deer in New York State, too."

"But they're hidden in the trees there. Here they're out in the open where you can see and really appreciate them."

They stopped on a small hill and left the truck to survey the land. It was like a patchwork quilt with fields of different shades of green spread out in all directions.

"Do you like it here?"

"Yes, it's nice. What is that bright yellow field?" she asked as she pointed to the south.

"That's canola, also known as rape seed."

Funny how her approval meant so much to him, but it did. She shivered in the breeze and, before he realized it, he had his arm around her, pulling her close to him to keep her warm. She stiffened for a second and then leaned into him. She fit against his side perfectly. His pulse thrummed in a happy rhythm.

She was safe here for a while, and maybe they had eluded the Creep. Perhaps they wouldn't have to worry about him anymore and she could find her way home. The thought of setting her loose gave his heart a tug. If he let her go, he might never see her again, and he wasn't quite ready for that to happen. He was foolish to keep her around, but he couldn't seem to release her.

He gave her shoulders a squeeze and headed back to the truck. "We best go and spend more time with Matt. He'll be up from his nap by now," Bruce suggested.

When they drove back through town, he stopped at his favorite spot and bought her ice cream. Like teens on a date, they sat in the truck with the frozen dessert and talked.

Tingles slid down his spine when she leaned over and wiped his face with a napkin to catch the ice cream that had run down his chin.

What would her lips taste like if he leaned over and kissed her? Would they be cold from the ice cream or warm like he remembered? Would they taste like the strawberry she was eating? Of course, they would.

These were dangerous thoughts that would lead to heartache. He started the truck and headed back to the ranch. Her lips were better left unexplored.

They drove the back roads and when they returned to the farm, supper was ready. They ate the rest of the stew and bannock, and all was well until Matt mentioned that the stew had buffalo meat in it. His family thought it was fun to fool a white guest. They couldn't do that with deer. It had a wild taste and people knew right away that they were eating something unfamiliar.

Amanda's eyes grew big and round. She covered her surprise, but Bruce knew she wouldn't have eaten it if she'd known. It tasted a lot like beef and many wouldn't notice that it wasn't. It was leaner, with less fat in it, better to have in the diet.

They all helped with cleanup then took their coffee out on the porch. They spent the evening in quiet conversation while Kohkom's rocker kept a steady beat on the worn planks.

Bruce steered the talk around to the Cree legends that his grandmother loved to tell. He wanted Amanda to hear them and understand a little of his native culture.

After some coaching, Kohkom said, "Long ago the Creator looked out over the perfect world He had made—the oceans, mountains, plains, deserts, lakes, and rivers and He was pleased. He looked upon the plants and trees and was happy at what He saw. Still, He felt there was something missing.

"There was no movement, nothing to enjoy the beauty He had created. So He made the animals, birds, creepers, and fish. He made them in all sizes, forms, colors, and shapes. As He watched them roam over Mother Earth, enjoying the beauty of His creations, He was pleased with all that He had done. Life continued on Mother Earth in perfect balance and harmony.

"Many moons passed and one day the animals, birds, creepers, and fish called out to their Creator. "We thank You for all that You have given us, for all the beauty that surrounds us. However, everything is so plentiful that we have nothing to do but wander here and there, with no purpose to our lives.

"The Creator gave great thought to this. After a while, He showed Himself again to his creations. He told them He would give them a weaker creature to take care of, to look after, and teach. This creature would not be so perfect as His other creations. It would come upon Mother Earth weak, small, and knowing nothing.

"So the Creator made man and woman and all His other creations were happy. Now they truly had a purpose in life—to care for these helpless humans, to teach them how to find food and shelter, and to show them the healing herbs.

"The humans, under the care of all, multiplied and grew to be many. Still the animals, birds, creepers, and fish took care of them. As the humans became stronger, they demanded more and more from their brothers. Finally, there came a day when a human man demanded more food than he needed, but the animal would not grant him his request. The man, in great anger, picked up a rock and killed the animal. From the dead animal, the man discovered that he could use the meat to feed himself and the skin to cover his body. The bones, claws, and teeth would be his trophies to show the other humans that now he was as smart as the animals.

"When he showed these things to the other humans, in their greed to have all that he had, they started killing all of their animal brothers around them.

"The Creator watched them all—humans, animals, birds, creepers, and fish. Finally, He called the remaining animals, birds, creepers, and fish to Him. The Creator told them that He had decided to take them all to His spirit home and leave the humans to rule over Mother Earth for a period of time until they recognized the error of their ways.

"The animals, knowing that the humans could not survive without them, begged the Creator to take pity on their human brothers and sisters.

"Because the animals showed compassion and pity for ones weaker and less wise than themselves, the Creator listened to their pleas and then said, 'Because you are good and have followed My ways, I will grant you your prayer. In order to protect you, I will no longer allow you to speak with humans, or guide and protect them. I will make you afraid of them so that you will no longer approach them. I will create a spirit animal to represent each of you. To this spirit animal, I will grant one gift that he may use. If humans live in a good and kind way and follow my path, they may ask Me for one of my spirit animals to guide and keep them on my path. This spirit animal will only come to humans who have a good heart.

"And so today, we seek our spirit keepers to learn how to be as kind and wise as our animal brothers. In seeking them, we wish to learn how to please the Creator, as the animals did before us."

Amanda sat so still during Kohkom's story her foot had gone to sleep. She rubbed at it, enthralled by Bruce's rich heritage. They believed in Creator God and strived to be good.

As the others went into the house for the night, Bruce asked if she'd like to go to the corrals for a walk before they went to the trailer. When they reached the corral, he grabbed her hand and they walked out the driveway, past the trees that ringed the property. The prairie had an earthy smell to it. It was dark where they stood beyond the yard lights.

"You okay, Buttercup?"

"Yes, I'm fine." It seemed strange that Bruce was always interested in how she was feeling. A warm fuzzy feeling surrounded her when he took the time to ask how she was. None of the men she had gone out with ever seemed to care or take notice of how she felt. He'd make some girl a caring husband someday.

"I loved your grandmother's story. I wish we could stay longer. I'd love to get to know your family better."

"I wish I could spend more time with my brother, too, but I have to continue on after church tomorrow to follow the schedule my boss agreed to when he set up the sale of the horses."

"It's so peaceful here. I could almost forget there is a whole other world out there." She sighed

"It is peaceful."

"I feel safe here. Do you think the Creep is still out there?"

"He could be looking for you, but I think he must have given up by now. We've been off his radar for two days. By the time we go back to the highway, he'll have returned to New York."

"I still can't figure out why he wanted me. Maybe he was looking for a different Amanda. My life is spent helping my mother with charity events and hanging out with my cousins and friends. I don't even cut people off in traffic." She grinned and Bruce smiled with her, the smile that sent shivers down her spine.

"Bruce, what's that?" She pointed to a spot in the sky that had turned a bluish green and came up from the horizon.

"That's what I brought you out here to see, Buttercup. That's the Northern Lights. They usually only last a few minutes, so let's just stay here and enjoy the show."

The color darkened to blue-green and rose in waves that moved and changed. Amanda grabbed Bruce's arm. "Oh, Bruce, they're amazing."

"Do you know they've been seen as far south as New Orleans?"

"Are you kidding? We never see them in New York."

"Probably because of all the lights. They would be obscured."

"What causes them?"

"I'm not sure, but it has something to do with gas particles from the sun. Sorry, I can't tell you more. I studied it in school, but I don't remember. That was quite a while ago."

"I could stay here all night and watch them."

"Too bad they usually only last a few minutes at a time."

Bruce was right. They were soon finished, and Amanda walked with him back to the trailer, a sense of loss in her chest. He held the door open for her.

"I'm going back to the house for a minute. I need to talk to Matt."

"Okay, goodnight." Her sense of loss doubled as Bruce walked away. His long shadow cast by the yard light.

Bruce left Amanda in the doorway. He could feel her gaze on him as he crossed the yard. The door to the RV didn't close until he was on the porch. Matt was alone in the kitchen having hot chocolate.

"Can I make you a cup, bro?"

"Sure." Bruce took a seat at the kitchen table. "I was hoping to catch you by yourself. I'm worried about you. What is going on with your health?"

"As you can probably tell from my color, the prognosis isn't good."

The green cast to Matt's skin was one of the first signs that had tipped Bruce off. Things weren't as rosy as the family had led him to believe.

"I don't honestly know how much longer I have, but I do know that I want you to have the ranch when I'm gone. With one stipulation, that you let Nola stay here on the ranch for as long as she wants."

"We'll see about that when the time comes. Nola is welcome to stay as long as she wants." He had a life he was quite happy with in New York State, but he wasn't about to get into an argument with his brother about it now.

Deep regret and sadness took Bruce's breath and strangled him. He'd never cried in front of another man, but he was close to it. Matt had had his back so many times when they were growing up. Bruce longed to have his now, but cancer was one thing he couldn't make go away. The situation was in God's hands and Bruce knew they were going to have to rely on God's wisdom. If Matt was to go soon, then they would have to make the best of the time he had left.

Bruce crossed the kitchen to the counter where Matt leaned. He grasped his brother in a manly hug. "I promise to watch over things, bro."

"I know you will. Just please watch over Nola and be good to her."

"You know I will."

"I have an envelope to give you with all of my financial info and my final wishes. Nola will be too torn up to think straight, so it'll fall to you to look after everything."

An hour later, envelope in hand, Bruce crossed the yard to the trailer. Amanda was sitting on the side of the bed, brushing her hair when he stepped in. She must have noticed how upset he was, because after he put the envelope away in the cupboard, she was standing behind him.

He turned and she wrapped her arms around his waist and held him in a warm hug. "I know how awful you must be feeling, Bruce. I lost my cousin last year to cancer," she said, her voice muffled against his neck.

He gave in to the hug and buried his face in her hair. Comfort and warmth washed over him in waves. When she lifted her face, he kissed her—the most natural thing in the world. She kissed him back and he lost himself in the sensations.

In the old days, he would have scooped her up in his arms and carried her to bed. He wanted to now. But he had made an oath to God that he wouldn't defile a woman in that way ever again. He would wait until he was married to enjoy passion with his bride.

He had to fight hard against his body's reaction to Amanda. She was so beautiful, inside and out. She fit so perfectly in his arms. However, his relationship with God was more important than a night with Amanda. He broke the kiss and stepped back, looking deep into her eyes. "Buttercup, you better head to bed, before I forget I'm a Christian who plans to wait 'til I marry."

She looked a little lost and disoriented as she slipped behind the curtain that separated the bed from the rest of the trailer. Thankful that she didn't argue, he took a long shower.

CHAPTER FOURTEEN

AMANDA SPENT HOURS lying awake wondering about the kiss. Bruce had kissed her breathless then acted as if he regretted it. She tried to stop thinking about it the next morning as she washed and got ready for church, but it still bothered her.

Nola loaned her an outfit to wear to church, and as she saw herself in the mirror she gasped, surprised at how pretty she looked. The dress, a stylish one in blue with accents in white, fit perfectly—the cabled sweater was soft white, like a cloud. It reminded her of purity. A week ago, she would never have enjoyed wearing another woman's discarded clothes, but now it was all right.

She picked up her purse and exited the RV to wait in the kitchen for Bruce. He was busy taking a shower and humming to himself when she clicked the door shut. In the corral, the horses neighed to one another. Swallows sat chatting on the electric wires that ran to the house.

Amanda passed her clutch to her left hand as she opened the door with her right. Why would that man put a tracking device in her purse? She couldn't ponder it now, but it still puzzled her that anyone would do something like that. It just didn't make sense.

Nola and Bruce's grandmother, dressed for church, looked chic in their Sunday best. Nola jumped up to pour Amanda a cup of coffee while Kohkom patted the seat beside her.

Amanda smiled and sat in the chair indicated. "I saw the Northern Lights last night for the first time. They're wonderful."

"Yes, child. They are the dancing spirits of our dead relatives. God's creation is beyond our imagining."

So true. Nature never ceased to amaze Amanda.

When she went to get her second cup of coffee, Bruce entered, a burst of cool morning air following in his wake. He looked handsome in his dressy cowboy shirt, pressed pants, and his Stetson. The fancy blue shirt brought out the blue in his eyes. Her breath caught as he bent to kiss his grandmother. So much love in the gesture, it sent a sizzle of emotion through her.

Her family was cold in comparison. Her mother would offer her cheek for a kiss and that was about the extent of her affection. Her dad would give hugs, but she had to ask for them. He would never be spontaneous.

She'd learned about love and loving more from her cousins who were demonstrative in their affection, freely hugging and kissing each other without restraint.

It'd felt so wonderful to be held in Bruce's arms. Safe, secure, with a measure of caring. It couldn't be called love. She didn't know him well enough—wasn't sure she wanted that. After all, he was a cowboy with no real social standing to speak of, and all of her life it had been drilled into her that she must seek a good match when the time came. To choose a husband within her class who met her parents' standards.

Her head said Bruce didn't measure up, but her heart sent a different message. Frightening and annoying, her inner battle upset her stomach.

Matt pulled his SUV up to the back door, and they filed out and entered the vehicle. Amanda sat in the back with Bruce and Nola. Bruce patted her hands where they lay in her lap.

"You okay, Buttercup?"

She smiled and said, "Yes, fine." So caring, it gripped her heart every time he showed her his loving nature.

A little nervous about going to his church, she took deep breaths and tried to stay calm. The one her family attended in New York looked like a cathedral compared to the Palmer's small, white clapboard building. When they pulled up to the door, Matt got out, opened her door for her, and then turned to the front passenger's side to help his grandmother out.

Bruce walked up the steps beside Amanda, taking his Stetson off as he entered the building. They did things differently here. No one ushered them to their seats. The choir didn't wear choir gowns. There was no soft organ music. A small band played praise choruses. The reverend wasn't wearing a priest's robe. Instead, he'd dressed in a suit that didn't even have a white collar.

They didn't sit or stand at the times she thought they should. It was all very confusing. She crossed her arms over her chest and sat quietly, enjoying the music. The words were sung with reverence and meaning directed toward Jesus and not so much God.

The biggest surprise came during the sermon.

The sermon was entitled 'Jesus is Waiting.' The pastor, as they called him instead of reverend, talked about having a relationship with Jesus. In all her experience of going to church every Sunday and sitting in the Vanderbilt pew, she'd never been asked to have a personal relationship with Jesus.

"Jesus is waiting for you," the pastor said. "He is a gentleman and will not go where He hasn't been invited. The Bible tells us that He stands at the door and knocks." He pointed to a lovely, old-fashioned picture of Jesus holding a lantern and knocking on a door. Amanda had seen that image before—it was familiar and it tugged at her heart.

"He knocks at our heart's door, waiting for us to invite Him in. Many times, we have excuses why we don't open the door to Him. My life changed when I let Him in. Yours would, too. No more drinking, no more bad habits. You would want to spend your time in different places, if you let Him in. You know, men. I'm looking at you. The bar is not a place Jesus wants you to spend your time. You would want to spend your time with family instead of partying."

Conviction stabbed Amanda's chest. It was an uncomfortable weight under her ribs. Her life was filled with parties and drinking. Jesus wouldn't be pleased, yet she'd never thought of it that way before.

"Jesus is waiting for you," The pastor said again, and he seemed to be saying it directly to her. She squirmed in her seat and looked to see what the people around her did. They listened, their full attention on the minister. Bruce looked contented, as if he'd already made a decision and let Jesus in. The odd person looked uncomfortable.

The pastor went on. "You need to let Him in. You will not regret it. He will change your life and you can have a relationship with Him. When you pray to Him, you will be on a higher level. You will be closer to Him than you've ever been. He will take care of you, like He never has before."

This message was so different from anything Amanda had ever heard. Church was just the place you showed up each Sunday to visit with your friends and go to brunch with them after the service. No one talked about making a personal commitment, to have Jesus in one's life, and making it real.

The pastor kept speaking and Amanda tried hard to listen. Listen for the first time in church, instead of watching what her neighbors in the pews did, and what they wore, and which eligible man they sat with. This pastor's message was sinking in and she wanted to understand.

"Jesus is waiting," he said again. "Will you let Him in today?"

The words rocked her to her very soul. Suddenly, she wanted that more than anything. Her pulse thrummed in her ears and she grabbed Bruce's hand. He squeezed it and bowed his head.

The pastor led them all in a prayer and Amanda joined them, truly wanting to change her life and find what these simple-living people had found.

The pastor's voice echoed out from the pulpit. "Heavenly Father, I ask that You help those who seek You today. Help them to let go of whatever is holding them back from surrendering to You. May they relax and let You take over. The Bible says in Jeremiah 29:11, You have a plan for us. A plan to help us and not to harm us. You want to give us hope and a future. Please, take over our lives and work out Your plan in us. We ask in Jesus' name because You love us, Lord. Amen."

Amanda felt something change inside her. She couldn't even describe it to herself. She only knew it was real.

After the service, they gathered in a back room for refreshments. A weight had lifted from under her ribs, and a joy she'd never experienced before took over. Bruce kept smiling at her as if he knew a secret, one they shared. If she'd won the lottery, she couldn't have been more happy and free.

While standing, drinking coffee and eating a cookie, a woman came to speak to Bruce. She was mildly flirty as she asked him how he was and what was new. A stab of jealousy rocked Amanda. Silly she would be jealous of a pretty lady talking to Bruce. She had no claim on him and she never could have, so being jealous was ridiculous.

She looked across the room, hoping to distract herself. Several people crowded around Matt. They were obviously concerned and probably asking about his treatments. To avoid the uncomfortable sensation brought on by the woman fawning over Bruce, Amanda wandered over to Matt and Nola.

Coffee time over, they all went back to the ranch in Matt's SUV. Amanda's heart ached as they stood in the yard to say good-bye. Her time with the Palmer family had been far too short, especially knowing this would be the last time she would see them. She hugged Bruce's grandmother tightly. Her cheeks were wet when they separated, and Kohkom wiped at the tears on Amanda's face.

"Thank you so much for sharing your bannock and corn ball recipes with me. I'll make them often and think of you. I enjoyed the legend you told us and will never forget it."

"The Spirit is with you now, child. Let Him lead you. I will see you again."

"I'm sorry, Kohkom, but I won't be back."

The old woman peered at her with knowledge in her gaze that was otherworldly. Then Amanda slid into the seat beside Bruce. He honked the horn and they pulled out of the yard. Amanda sensed she was leaving family behind.

They passed through Indian Head on their way back to the TransCanada highway. Bruce stopped long enough to pick up a few essential groceries, gas up, and then they were off again.

The day was warm and Amanda opened her window a couple of inches. The hum of the tires on the pavement relaxed her. Bruce turned the radio to his country music. Instead of it grating on her nerves, Amanda started to like the ballads and the rock beat of some of the songs.

BRUCE SET THE cruise control to the speed limit and sat back to enjoy the afternoon drive. He thought about what had happened earlier and realized that God had a plan for his life with Amanda, and because she'd been in church with him that morning, her whole life would be different. When she'd grabbed his hand, he knew the Spirit had spoken to her, and she'd made a decision. The annoying moments he'd spent with her when they had first met had been worth it.

Why hadn't she asked to go home? He was certain that the threat from the Creep was over. It didn't matter to him. He was quite content to take her with him and drop her off in New York when he got back. Easy to look at, there was a radiance about her that hadn't been there before.

The hardest thing he'd ever done had been to leave his brother. They'd pulled each other out of so many scrapes when they were kids. Bruce swallowed the lump forming in his throat and tried not to dwell on it. The talk he'd had in private with Nola didn't give him much hope. According to the doctors, the chemo wasn't keeping up with the progression of the cancer. Although no one was saying it aloud, it seemed it wouldn't be too much longer before Matt would end up in the hospital for the last time.

The RV in front of Bruce slowed down to turn into a gas station. Bruce checked his mirror before changing lanes to go around him. That's when something sinister caught his attention.

No, please don't tell me!

CHAPTER FIFTEEN

THE SEMI WAS three cars back and pulling into the passing lane. Fear and anger shot through Bruce.

Now what?

"The Creep is back." His words ricocheted in the small space of the cab, sending a shiver down his spine. He hated to say it and ruin their day, but there was no sense in waiting. Amanda had to know, and they needed to strategize.

Bruce had hoped they'd lost him, and the Creep had given up and crawled back under his rock. He must have driven up and down the highway looking for them for the past two days while they were staying with his family.

Amanda turned to him. "What are we going to do?" Her face had lost color and her eyes were the size of dinner plates.

"What did you ever do to get this guy so riled up?"

"I don't understand," she wailed. "I can't imagine what he wants."

Anger bubbled up. "That's it. I've had enough. I'm pulling off at the next gas station to call the cops."

"Yes. Let's." She turned to check the mirror again. "Let him explain his behavior to the police. They can figure out why he won't leave us alone."

Bruce smiled at what she'd said. *Leave us alone.* He planned to do whatever it took to keep her safe and get her home to Monica.

He raced ahead and pulled into the first gas station with an old-fashion phone booth. Bruce would have liked it located inside the station, but this would have to do. He left the engine running and jumped out, quarters in hand, to make the call. He scrambled to get the booth's door open—it was old and rusted.

"Nobody uses this thing anymore, obviously. Everyone has cell phones except me," he mumbled under his breath. His hands shook as he piled in the coins. Then realized to call 911 he didn't need them. He cleared the machine and started again.

A woman's voice said, "911, what is the nature of your emergency?"

"I have someone stalking me."

He had no sooner spoken the words when the gravel at the edge of the lot crunched. The monstrous truck headed straight for him, its engine roaring.

He gasped, unable to comprehend what he saw for a split second. When it registered that he intended to keep coming, Bruce jumped.

The phone dropped, dangling on its tether. He fell. His knees hit hard and he skidded in the gravel. Amanda's scream clenched his chest and his heart stopped. The truck continued, and the sound of the phone booth splintering terrified him. The sound of glass shattering and wood and metal breaking registered an eight on Bruce's personal Richter scale. His head hit the ground with a thump. His ears rang as he tried to rise. Glass lay all around him. Amanda screamed his name repeatedly as she bent at his side, pulling his arm to help him to his feet.

"Bruce get up, get up! He's coming back."

The words garbled in his mind, but the urgency in her voice had him on his feet. With his knees stinging and head woozy, she dragged him to the truck. He fell into the passenger seat and the door slammed behind him. Half on the floor between the two seats, he heard her get in and they roared out of the lot. When he sat up, he saw several patrons of the café come out to see what was going on, mouths gaping.

The semi was in hot pursuit.

Fear sizzled through Bruce's veins.

This guy wanted them dead!

Bruce lay helpless as Amanda drove. Because her hands shook so badly, the truck weaved. They hit the dirt on the side of the pavement a couple of times, and Bruce was sure she would spin out. His body ached from all the abuse.

Unable to assist, he prayed, "Heavenly Father, we need Your help." The words came out of his mouth and Amanda turned to him. Her eyes were round orbs, like saucers. He patted her arm to give her comfort. He was afraid to speak, because if he did, she'd hear the fear in his voice and he didn't want to spook her while she drove.

Bruce kept checking to see what the semi was doing. He'd pulled up behind them, coming up close, then he'd drop back and fall a short way behind.

Taunting them.

It was a matter of life or death now, and Amanda was driving. She was in top gear, so he didn't have to worry about her shifting. But she wasn't experienced with standard shift, and that worried him. If the Creep bunted her from behind, would she recover and keep them on the road? He doubted it. She was panicked and shaking.

He took control of his voice and tried to calm her. "Mandy, you're doing fine. Just keep us on our side of the highway and we'll be all right." He hoped the wink he gave helped.

"I can't die, Bruce. Monica needs me."

So that's what she was thinking about. Good, she had the will to fight. That's what he needed to know. The desire to get back to Monica would help her to keep a cool head.

He tried to think what he might do to get away from the Creep. If only there was a police station along the highway, but he grew up here and knew they were all nicely tucked in the towns. If he were driving, he'd make his way to the police station. But with his knees still stinging from his fall, he wasn't sure how fast he could run. If they got into town, he wondered if Amanda could gear down for corners or would stall, leaving them sitting ducks for the semi to run them over.

They needed a miracle. He prayed as hard as he knew how for protection and guidance. Amanda's lips were moving.

She was praying, too.

CHAPTER SIXTEEN

AMANDA TRAMPED ON the gas and passed an SUV. She wanted to stop and confront the man in the semi, but thoughts of Monica without a mom and dad stopped her. She didn't want her brought up as she had been, left alone with nannies or sent off to an expensive boarding school.

She wanted to give up, but she also had to think about Bruce, the man with the soft, loving eyes when he looked at her. Eyes that shot fire when angry. The cowboy who couldn't toss her out though he'd clearly wanted to when he'd found her hiding in his truck.

She had to go on and keep this man, who'd been so good to her, safe. There had to be a way to get rid of the Creep.

"Bruce, what are we going to do?"

"I've been thinking on that. Once we get to the mountains, there'll be roads where the semi won't be able to follow us."

"The mountains are still a long way off, aren't they?"

"Yah, I know, and we need to switch drivers. We're gettin' low on cash, too. I'm thinkin' if we find a pool hall, I may be able to make us some money. That's if you'll let me use what you have left in that fancy wallet of yours." When she hesitated, he asked, "Do you play pool?"

"No." After a moment, she said, "You can have my money."

When they reached Medicine Hat, Alberta, Bruce yelled, "Turn here."

Amanda swung onto a city street and the semi blew past. Bruce laughed and she let out a sigh. She made a few more turns just to make sure he was gone then pulled into a gas station.

They refuelled and Bruce said, "That's all my cash." Bruce swallowed the lump in his throat. "The guy inside the gas station told me where to find the pool hall. Maybe I can make us some money."

In his younger days, Bruce had spent many hours playing pool with his friends. He was good enough to beat anyone who came through the door. Hopefully, he'd make enough cash to get them to Seattle where his boss would wire him money to buy the horses and to make the return trip.

After turning into the lot and parking, he exited and adjusted his Stetson to the right angle. The passenger door slammed and he swung back to see Amanda had left the truck.

"What are you doin'?"

With a coquettish grin, Amanda said, "Coming with you."

"Oh, no, you're not."

"Why?"

"A pool hall is no place for a lady like you."

She seemed affronted as she said, "I'm coming," then swept past him with her nose in the air.

She was one strong-willed woman. He gave up arguing with her. With his head shaking and his boots kicking up dust, he followed her.

It was late afternoon and there weren't many patrons in the dimly lit room. Two of the four tables had players.

Bruce ordered a soft drink for him and Amanda, and studied the men playing pool. The balls rattled against the rails and clunked into the leather pockets. He decided he could beat the burly one and the skinny guy.

When they finished their game, he approached them. "How about we play?"

The burly one eyed him. "Sure, why not?"

The skinny guy asked, "Your woman wanta play, too?"

Bruce was about to say no when Amanda stepped forward, a pool cue in her hand.

Oh, no. Pull-ease.

Too late. Burly was racking up the balls. He only hoped they didn't lose too much of the money left in Amanda's fancy diamond wallet.

They settled on a wager and the game began.

Burly was good, sinking balls right and left. Skinny made a couple of mistakes. That helped.

Bruce gave a good showing, but it had been a long time since he'd played, and he wasn't as good as he remembered. Then Amanda took over the table. She sank everything in sight—hard, impossible shots.

Bruce gaped as the balls plopped into one hole after another. Amanda banked off the sides as if that was easy.

Soon the game was over and Burly handed over the money. Bill after bill slapped Bruce's palm. Amanda had tripled their money. As they left the building, Bruce held the door open and asked, "I thought you had never played pool before?"

She met his gaze with a grin. "I haven't. My daddy called it billiards. We have a table in the games room and we played with a different set of colored balls."

Bruce huffed and rolled his eyes as he let the door shut behind them. This woman was one surprise after another. Not only beautiful and smart, but she had untold talents, too. Now if he could just keep her safe and get her back to her baby girl.

They bought some food and headed back out onto the highway.

"What's the plan now?" Amanda asked.

"I'm going to cross from Alberta into Montana, then through the mountains, and on to a ranch outside Seattle. I'll pick up the horses for my boss then head back home."

"Do you think the Creep will find us again?"

"Too many times I've thought that we were rid of him, and he showed up again. I'm not making any more predictions."

"Yes. I see what you mean. He's like a bad smell. Just keeps turning up."

Bruce mentally kicked himself. Why hadn't he gone to the police when he'd had the chance? Did Amanda have his mind so tied up in knots that he'd forget something that important? Man, he felt stupid.

No doubt now, the guy was out for blood. If Bruce hadn't jumped, he would have been smashed to bits like the phone booth.

A shiver went down his spine as he envisioned the glass and debris scattered in the semi's wake. Small particles of what was once a wooden structure left in the dust.

"Oh, goodness, no!" Amanda grabbed his arm and pointed. "That's him on the right, parked in that driveway."

Cold fear took Bruce's breath as he recognized the semi's filthy trailer, so dirty the writing on its side was indistinguishable.

"Look at that, he must have hit a deer. That looks like dried blood on the bumper." Bruce leaned forward.

Amanda let out a sob.

"Sorry. I shouldn't have said anything," Bruce apologized as he tramped on the gas and sped by the huge idling truck.

"Here he comes." Amanda gasped.

Bruce's heart pounded as he raced ahead.

This isn't funny anymore.

Night was falling and they had the border to cross.

The hours passed with them outrunning the big rig, but they weren't able to lose him when they turned south off the TransCanada.

He's playing with us again. He's waiting to catch us on a mountain pass and force us over the side. His knuckles turned white, and he wiped his damp hands on his jeans.

He glanced down at the woman asleep against his shoulder. Her messy, blonde hair fanned across her cheek. Warmth spread through him as he watched the beautiful girl sleep. How had she become so dear to him? When they'd first met, she could be so annoying. What was he doing having these feelings for a person who soared so high above him socially? Any relationship with her would fail and he would be heartbroken.

He'd like to know what she had done to make this guy decide to kill the two of them. Picking up strangers could be dangerous and, man, he'd found that out the hard way. It was obvious the Creep wanted him dead. Was he a jealous lover? A fixated psychopath? Did he want to punish her for something?

One thing for sure, Bruce wouldn't let anything happen to her. He had to get to the mountains and lose this guy. Or maybe he'd lose him at the border between Canada and the States.

If the Creep would just cool it until he reached the US, the guards would stop him.

CHAPTER SEVENTEEN

AMANDA ROCKED MONICA gently in her arms. Her angel eyes fluttered closed as she fell asleep.

She jerked awake.

She'd been dreaming. Her head lay against the soft cotton of Bruce's shirt. A line of cars had stopped in front of them. A stream of red lights lit the dark, rainy night.

"Where are we?" she asked, rubbing at her eyes.

"Sweetgrass border crossing."

"I have to hide." Her heart sped up and her breath caught in her throat.

"No, we're going in and talking to the guards and get the Creep arrested."

"But, Bruce, I don't have papers."

"It just means we have to wait while they verify your citizenship. With your fancy name that shouldn't take long."

They argued as the line slowly moved forward, one vehicle at a time.

"Where's the Creep?"

"He was a few cars back. In this rain, I've lost sight of him. But once we talk to the border guards, he should be arrested or at least detained."

Doubt had her crossing her arms and chewing her lip. This might not go the way Bruce planned.

The truck moved up the line, closer to the guardhouse, and Amanda thought of all that might go wrong. What if they didn't believe her when she told them who she was? What if they wanted to strip-search her? What if they didn't believe Bruce and they let the Creep go through?

When they pulled up to the guardhouse, she had worked herself up into a panic.

Please, let us get through without a lot of fuss.

Bruce stopped the truck and wound down the window. A stern-faced man stepped into view. His vigilant eyes scanned from person to person then focused on their truck.

"Sir, we want to report an attempt on our life, and my friend here will need to prove her identity to cross the border."

"You'll need to see an RCMP officer to report a crime in Canada. Pull over into lane three, and I'll have someone escort you inside to take your statement."

After giving their names, Bruce parked the truck and trailer. He leaned over and grabbed her hand. "It's going to be all right, Buttercup. We're in this together."

Relief washed over her. She needed to hear that.

Rain splashed against the windshield while they waited until a Royal Canadian Mounted police officer approached the truck. With RCMP emblazoned on his sleeve, he looked sharp in his uniform.

"Mr. Palmer and Miss Vanderbilt?" he asked.

They both nodded.

"Come inside with me, please."

Amanda trembled as they left the truck and dashed after the police officer through the rain. They were ushered into a brightly lit room with a mirror running along one cinder-block wall. Amanda took a shaky breath and tried to relax.

"I'm Constable Grieves and I'll be taking your statement," he said, shaking each of their hands. "Now, Mr. Palmer, you need to report an attempted murder?"

Bruce leaned forward. "Yes, sir. We stopped at a gas station to use the phone to call 911. The semi that has been harassing us and tried to bump us off the road sped onto the lot and smashed the phone booth I was in. Lucky I spotted him in time and jumped, or I'd be dead."

"What can you tell me about the truck?"

"It's an old semi tanker, so dirty we couldn't read the writing on the side. The license plate is obscured by dirt. The cab appears black or possibly navy."

Constable Grieves scribbled notes as Bruce recalled the incident. Grieves looked to Amanda and she nodded her affirmation from time to time.

"Why would this man be stalking you?"

Amanda spoke up, telling him about the party, the attack, and the GPS device they'd found in her clutch.

"You have no idea why he's following you or why he wants to harm you?"

Amanda and Bruce said no in unison.

"We wondered if he wants to kidnap me because my parents are rich. There are two men involved, because the man who dropped the GPS into my bag is not the one chasing us. The one chasing us is the man in the mask who accosted me outside in the garden. I recognize his eyes and the way his brows grow together in the middle. Unibrow, I think it's called."

After taking a description of both men, Constable Grieves said, "Okay, I'll put a hold on the truck here at the border and an APB on my side." He stood and shook hands. "Miss Vanderbilt, come with me. I'll find a US border guard to help you with your paperwork."

Bruce held her hand as they dashed back through the rain to the American guardhouse. She was shown to a small room. Her pulse thrummed madly in her ears. Amanda took some deep breaths. Proving who she was and convincing them might become an ordeal. Her parents were out of the country, so she wondered how she'd convince them without her ID.

The room was overly warm, and she wished she could leave, or at least have Bruce sit with her. She had come to rely on the strength he projected, and his grin would be a welcome sight right now. It was surprising how she relied on him and how fond of him she had become.

The door clicked open and a burly little man in a dark uniform slipped in. He dropped a sheaf of papers on the table and ran his hand over his balding head.

"Ms. Vanderbilt, I'm Officer Jones. I understand you need my help to cross into the United States."

Her hands shook and she tried to settle them in her lap. She swallowed hard while Officer Jones shuffled his documents.

He took her information then turned to a computer on his right and typed. Amanda's driver's license popped up on the screen. She cringed at the terrible photo. The man compared the picture to her and nodded. He soon had her birth certificate and confirmation of address on the screen. He asked her to sign her name and compared her signature to the one on her license.

Officer Jones closed the computer screen, grabbed the papers that she had signed, and stood. "Next time be sure and bring your ID with you." With that said, he walked out of the room, leaving Amanda feeling a little wide eyed.

She walked down the hallway to find Bruce. She found him waiting in the entrance foyer. She must have looked forlorn, or shell-shocked, or something, because he stood and embraced her.

"You okay?" he whispered into her ear.

She nodded and held tight for a moment. "I was really scared." Authority figures had always been frightening for her, starting with her parents. They'd used intimidation with no warmth when disciplining her as a child.

Bruce kept his arm wrapped around her shoulders as he walked with her to the truck.

"It's over now, Buttercup. We can go."

She allowed herself a sigh of relief as she sank onto the seat. "Bruce, do you think they have him stopped?"

"They told me he hadn't come through the line while we were here, but he may have stopped for something to eat or for gas. Don't worry. They're waiting for him. They'll nab him when he tries to cross." Bruce patted her hand and she tried to return his smile.

CHAPTER EIGHTEEN

AMANDA HUGGED HERSELF as Bruce drove down Highway 15 in the drizzle. She watched the wipers slap the rain away. Things were okay. Bruce had made sure the Creep was no longer a threat and she could relax.

If only Monica was with her.

Tears stung her eyes every time she thought of her dear, sweet baby—if only Brad had lived to see her grow up.

She remembered her grandmother saying regrets were a dime a dozen these days. She was right. Regrets made tears gather in her eyes and threaten to spill onto her cheeks.

She noticed the difference between the way her parents treated her and the way Bruce made her an equal, discussing things with her, serious things, whereas her parents only expected her to look pretty, say and do the right things, and associate with only the best people.

Because Bruce's family owned a farm didn't make them less in her eyes. Spending time with the Palmers, seeing the love and care they felt for one another, made her think about the many times she had felt alone. Lonely, even when her parents were home. Not a situation she wanted to return to. When she was with Bruce she was alive, an adult, no longer a pampered princess but a real woman. He trusted her to drive the truck when her parents didn't even trust her with mundane things.

She needed to concentrate on the future—a healthy life for herself and Monica. She needed to make a life away from her parents and their influence. She had relied on Vanderbilt money long enough. When she got home, she'd find a job so she'd be able to be home every night. No boarding schools or months left in the care of nannies for her daughter.

Then she'd look for a good place where little girls grew up safe and happy, a small town with a low crime rate. A place where everyone knew each other and people looked out for one another. They could attend a church like the one Bruce grew up in at Indian Head—friendly and nurturing. And maybe, someday, she'd find a man like Bruce—gentle, truthful, protective, strong, hardworking, good looking, and dependable. She stole a glance at him. The lights from the dash gave his face a greenish glow.

Was she falling for him?

She gasped.

No she wasn't. Well, she didn't think she was, even though he was an amazing person.

Bruce belonged on a ranch like the one at Indian Head. He was relaxed there. A cowboy with his cattle and horses. He would not fit into the Vanderbilt world.

Bruce took his gaze from the road for a moment and smiled at her. "You okay, Buttercup?"

Her heart lit up and she smiled in answer. "Thanks, cowboy. I'm fine now."

"It's a relief. Isn't it?" He patted the cold hand in her lap with his warm one.

"Yes. I'm going to stop worrying and let the police deal with him."

"We'll pick up the horses for my boss and head for New York."

Amanda smiled up at Bruce and gave his hand a squeeze.

Home had always meant the Vanderbilt mansion, but since meeting Kohkom and the rest of Bruce's family, the word 'home' brought visions of Kohkom making bannock over a fire in the yard, and Nola laughing as she told her it could be baked in the oven. Bruce wiping at tears after hugging his too-thin brother.

The ranch at Indian Head was a true home where love lived and people cared.

"Help me watch for a trailer park and we'll stop for the night." Bruce's voice broke through her thoughts.

Amanda must have fallen asleep, because the next she knew she was in Bruce's arms, being carried to the trailer. Her head lolled against his shoulder.

"What are you doing?" she whispered.

"I'm putting you to bed, sleepy head."

She put her arms around his neck and cuddled in for the ride to the bunk. He settled her in the bed and covered her, whispering goodnight as he tucked blankets under her chin. Trusting all was well, she surrendered to the dream she'd been having when he carried her.

BRUCE LINGERED BY the sleeping woman who had become so precious to him. Her golden hair splayed on the pillow. Her curled lashes lay on her pink cheeks. Her kissable lips in a sleepy pout. Her chin jutting out at a proud angle.

If only she were some farmer's daughter or a working class girl that could be in his life. But, no, she was extreme high society, way beyond his class. Look, but don't touch.

He'd have to enjoy the time he had left with her—one day to pick up the horses and four days to ride back to New York. He'd make the best of them, saving up memories to take him through the lonely years ahead.

CHAPTER NINETEEN

Bruce had bacon and eggs frying when Amanda woke. She'd slept in her clothes. The border crossing anxiety had knocked the stuffing out of her. Grateful to Bruce for letting her sleep, she said, "Morning."

"Hey, you're awake."

She rubbed at her sleepy eyes and asked, "Where to today?"

After flipping the eggs, Bruce turned to her. "We're going across Highway 200 to catch I 90 into Missoula. I'm hoping to gas up and buy groceries for our trek through the mountains. It should be smooth sailing right to the ranch, now that the Creep is gone. You can relax and enjoy the scenery. It should be beautiful. You may even see some wildlife along the road."

Amanda hopped out of the bunk and headed to the washroom, a happy song in her heart.

By mid-morning, they'd left Missoula. Bruce had a country station playing on the radio. Amanda smiled, she was beginning to recognize the songs and hum along. She sang a couple of lines with the radio and soon Bruce joined in. He had a wonderful voice—deep, rich, and on key. A shiver of delight passed through her. Their voices blended together perfectly. She had always wished for a male singing partner who could harmonize with her.

They passed into the Clearwater National Forest. Huge boulders lay among the trees. Mountains in the distance appeared blue. Amanda gasped. She'd never seen such high mountains before. She was used to Lake Placid, which was small in comparison. Small, wispy clouds hung over a lake as they drove by.

They came around a bend and Bruce slammed on the brakes. A huge moose stood still in the middle of the road. He eyed them but didn't move. Bruce blasted the horn twice and the large beast continued to stare. He reminded Amanda of a cow chewing its cud.

Suddenly a very loud air horn sounded behind them. Birds scattered out of the nearby pines and the moose sauntered off the road.

"Please, don't tell me. Look, is that the Creep?" he asked as he stared into the side mirror.

Fear slammed her heart. "No, it can't be. They promised to stop him at the border."

Tires squealed as the truck and trailer leapt forward when Bruce hit the gas pedal. Amanda's knee banged the gearshift on the floor beside her. She located a semi in the side mirror that appeared dirty and unkempt like the Creep's. "It really looks like him. How could it be?" Her voice trembled with the fear she refused to admit.

"The only way it's him is if he turned back at the border and took a different crossing while we took so much time reporting at Sweetgrass. He may have turned back to Whitlash or gone on to Del Bonita. I saw them on the map when I decided where we should cross. Will this never end?"

"Well, I've had enough. I'm reporting to the next police office we come to. We should have bought another cell phone."

"There will be no signal when we get into the mountains," he grumbled.

Amanda's breathing had become rapid and shallow. Deep breaths calmed her, but her hands shook as she reached for the map. "We're heading right into the mountains now. The roads are going to become steep and winding."

"Yes, and some of the highway will be along the edge, overlooking huge, hundred-foot drops."

Amanda closed her eyes and prayed. Please, let that not be him behind us and, if it is, please, please, keep us safe. Heavenly Father, I really need to get home to Monica.

Monica with her dad's sweet smile. Grandmee Vanderbilt's blue eyes. Amanda's heart caught at her daughter's name for her favorite grandmother. Oh, how she missed her. She had to return to her.

Bruce drove like a maniac, trying to put distance between them and the semi. Amanda's hands white-knuckled the seat.

"I think it's him. He's speeding up when I do and hanging back when I slow for the curves." Concern peppered Bruce's words.

"It sure looks like the same truck. I can't believe he came through the border."

"Just his dumb luck, I guess, choosing a different route while we took time to explain things. We have gas and food to get through the mountains, but I don't know what will happen when we have to stop to pick up the horses. If he is willing to run us down in a public place, he won't think twice to come into the yard while we're trying to load the horses."

Amanda caught Bruce's gaze. "I'm so sorry. I had no intention of putting you in any danger. This is so crazy."

"Like I said before, we're in this together now, Buttercup. We'll see it through as a team."

As the day wore on, Amanda's stomach began to burn with tension. The crackers Bruce offered did little to dampen the pain. Bruce held her hand for a while and that helped more than the food, but he soon needed both hands as they passed through the hairpin turns.

"Is that snow I see on those peaks?" Amanda asked.

"Yes. When we cross the divide in the mountains, the roads will likely be covered in snow. The elevation will be high and it will be cold enough for snow. We could even head into a snowstorm up there."

The mountain divide. What could she remember of it? From the primary grades, she remembered learning about it being the highest point in the Rocky Mountains, and all the water on the west side of the mountain flowed into the Pacific Ocean. The streams and rivers on the east side of the highest point flowed eastward toward the Atlantic Ocean. And, yes, it was high enough for there to be snow on the roads all year round.

She fumbled with the dial on the radio, trying to find a radio station that would give a weather report. If they were in for a bad time of it, she wanted to know.

Bruce grabbed her hand again, and the feelings she had for him snatched her breath. He would keep her safe, or at least try his best. His eyes shone with the unspoken promise.

When had this happened, this trusting, caring relationship between them? It sure hadn't been there in the beginning.

CHAPTER TWENTY

STATIC BLARED AS Amanda searched for a nearby station with a weather report. When she found one, the news wasn't good. Snow and wind were expected in the higher elevations overnight, with dropping temperatures.

"That is not what I wanted to hear," Bruce quipped. "We better skip lunch and drive on. Maybe we can get through the mountains before the storm hits."

The scenery changed as they climbed from foothills into the mountains. Amanda glanced in the side mirror, keeping an eye on the semi they'd spotted earlier. She would not believe it was the Creep. They'd stopped him at the border, but something about the truck following them now sent frissons of worry through her.

A half-hour before they reached the summit, the weather changed. A bank of dark clouds met them, and soon a sheet of snow fell, reducing visibility. The wipers slapped as fast as they would go, but it was impossible to see clearly. If someone parked on the side of the pavement, they'd hit them before seeing them.

"We need to get off this highway. I can't see. It's getting too dangerous," Bruce said through clenched teeth.

"I just thought the same thing."

"Good. We agree. Take shelter for a while."

They drove on until Bruce found a secondary road. He pulled off onto a farmer's field and cut the engine. "We should be safe here off the highway. We'll have a late lunch and pray this lets up, so we can go on before dark."

Amanda gathered empty wrappers and cans to carry back to the RV with her. She knew Bruce preferred things tidy. She thought about the maids at home and how much she had left behind every day for them to pick up. She'd have to change that when she returned to New York. No more making messes and expecting others to deal with them.

Bruce tried lighting the stove. He slammed the matches down on the counter and went outside. When he came back a few minutes later, he was angry. "We're out of propane. We can't stay here."

"I can go without something hot to eat."

"We need propane for the furnace."

"Oh." Her cheeks heated.

"Come on, we have to find a place to ride this out." He left her standing, and she had no other option but to follow him. After gathering her pride, she marched to the truck and buckled herself in.

Fifteen minutes down the road, Bruce found a driveway and turned in. Hemmed in with trees, they travelled the tight laneway. They exited the forest into a cleared area with a modern log cabin— an A-frame with lots of space. Snow swirled in the clearing. Amanda suspected they were high on a cliff, allowing the wind to howl into the opening. With the snow still falling in sheets, it became impossible to see the valley below.

"I'm going to see if we can get in." Bruce stepped out of the truck and was soon lost in a swirl of snow. At times, the snow slowed enough that she saw the building, but Bruce had disappeared. Minutes ticked by. The heat blasting from the truck's heater comforted her. Considerably colder at this elevation, she pulled Bruce's coat on and adjusted the collar high around her neck.

They'd have to be careful to leave things as they found them in the cabin. She didn't want to do anything illegal. Breaking in to survive a storm was acceptable in her mind as long as they left a note, some money to cover any food they might use, and didn't damage anything. The wind howled like a banshee through the trees, and snow was driven sideways through the clearing. Bruce reappeared, plowing through snow up to his knees. He flung the truck door open and jumped in.

"I opened the back door. We're going to owe the owner a new windowpane, though. Luckily, it's a small one. I turned the furnace up. They had it set only high enough so the pipes don't freeze. It'll take a while for it to get to room temperature."

"Thanks," she whispered.

"We'll carry our own food in and use as much of our own supplies, like towels and bedding, as we can."

"Okay." She started making a mental list of what they would need for an overnight stay. Hopefully, there was a tub. She wanted a good long soak.

When they had gathered up everything they needed, Bruce led the way to the back door. Amanda kept her coat on for the first hour, waiting for the cabin to warm up.

Bruce had found the generator earlier, powering up the lights and the kitchen appliances. Within minutes, the kettle whistled. Amanda found tea bags and mugs in the cupboards. To help take the damp chill out of the air, Bruce brought in wood and kindling and soon had a blaze started in the stone fireplace.

They sat on the couch in front of the fire, enjoying their hot tea. Bruce stretched his legs toward the heat. It didn't take long before steam rose from the bottom edge of his pants where snow had clung and melted from his walk through the deep snow.

"One thing about this cabin, if that was the Creep following, he can't get the semi in here. The laneway is too narrow."

The muscles in her stomach tightened. "Was that him behind us? If it's him, how did he cross the border?"

"The only way it could be him is if he crossed at another crossing while we were explaining about your lack of documents."

She swallowed and said, "I was so sure we were safe now."

He grabbed her hand and gave it a reassuring squeeze. "We are. Please, don't fret."

BRUCE KICKED HIMSELF for speaking when the worry lines deepened on her brow. He felt so stupid that he had been the one who put them there. It'd be best to get her mind on something else. "The water should be warm now. Did you want a shower?"

"I'd love a long soak in the tub, if there is one."

"Yes, there is. Please, go ahead take all the time you need. I'm going to check out the CD collection, put on some music, and relax."

Amanda grabbed some towels and a face cloth and headed down the hallway to the bathroom. He couldn't help his reaction to the thought of her in the water. If this had been earlier in his life, he would be asking if he could scrub her back, but he erased those thoughts, determined to be the Christian gentleman he longed to be. Matt's illness had brought him up short to see the evil way he'd been living, and he wanted to live now with God at the center of his life.

Bruce turned up the volume on the CD player to drown out the splashing and humming coming from the bathroom down the hall. He wasn't sure they had eluded the Creep. The semi that followed several cars behind them had looked far too familiar. He wished he knew what the man wanted. Would he try to hurt Amanda? Or kidnap her? Or what? She didn't seem to have a clear idea what he wanted. That made it harder for him to make a plan to protect her.

One thing was certain, the creep would have to come through him to get her. Amanda was too precious to him to let anything happen to her now.

Amanda came out of the washroom with her hair wet, curly, and tousled. He let out a loud sigh. This would be a long evening. By the time he finished his shower, Amanda had prepared sandwiches and hot chocolate.

They sat together on the couch in companionable silence as they ate.

"Tell me about growing up in your home. What was it like?" she asked as she popped an olive in her mouth.

Olives were a fancy item that his family had at parties, not something they ate every day. Amanda seemed to want them with every meal. In his daily life, they were far too expensive to have all the time.

"I grew up at Indian Head on the farm. My dad would come into the room Matt and I shared and wake us at dawn. If we didn't get up right away, he'd put his knees on the bed and tussle with us, messing our hair and tickling us with his cold hands. We'd take turns in the bathroom then go downstairs for breakfast. Mom would be there in her bathrobe, making oatmeal cereal. She'd let us sprinkle brown sugar on it. Kohkom would already be up, sitting at the end of the table with her coffee. On weekends, we had bacon and eggs or home-fried potatoes and sausages. Saturdays were a work day on the farm for Matt and me, so we ate hardy to see us through the morning's labor."

"What would you do?"

"Haul bales, fix fences, help Mom in her garden. Plus our regular chores like milking and feeding the animals." By her expression, he could tell she wasn't accustomed to all that work and thought it excessive. "What was your childhood like?"

"I played with the servants' children when I was small. Then I visited with my cousins. My parents weren't home often, so my uncle's family took us places like the water park or the beach. We spent summers at Kennebunkport and I learned to sail. That was my favorite time because I would be with both my mother and father."

"It sounds lonely."

"Oh, they made sure I had everything I wanted, but their priorities were elsewhere. It was frivolous and often empty. I promised myself I would always be in my child's life. So far I've kept that promise to Monica."

"You'd like to have more kids?"

She smiled. "Someday. How about you? You want children?"

Now she'd made him uncomfortable. He gulped and said, "I'm content as a loner. But lately I have to admit, a family and a farm of my own would be nice."

Bruce marveled at how easy this woman was to talk to, not like Julia. No subject was taboo, and they talked for hours. The longer he was with her the more attracted to her he became. It hurt that it would end and they would have to part.

The fire had died down and Amanda began to yawn.

"We better get some sleep," he suggested. "I'll go out and get more wood, then lock up." A good night kiss would have been nice, but he thought he had better not start something he could never finish. She put her cup in the sink and disappeared into the first bedroom.

Worry held his chest in its grip and he rushed back into the cabin with an armload of logs. He dropped them on the hearth and hurried to lock the door. He'd seen fresh boot prints in the snow.

They weren't alone.

CHAPTER TWENTY-ONE

WIND HOWLED ALL night. Bruce slept fitfully. When the sun came up, he was eager to leave. The thought that they weren't alone had nagged him all night. They tidied up. He checked the boss's instructions for the directions to the horse ranch, left money for the broken window, and packed a breakfast to eat in the truck.

The going would be rough until they made it to the highway. A couple of deep breaths relieved the tension building up in his stomach while he waited to see if they would make it out of the tree-sheltered laneway. They plowed snow most of the way from the cabin. Amanda let out a sigh when they turned onto the freshly cleared pavement and headed down the mountain.

"Oh, no. Not again." Bruce's voice broke the silence. Stress and anger rang in the truck cab.

"What?" Amanda gasped and she grabbed his arm.

"He's here! He's back."

"What? Who?"

"The Creep. I just saw the dirty, filthy truck behind us. He's a ways behind, but it's him."

Frown lines marred Amanda's forehead and dread turned his stomach sour. "How can that be?"

"I don't know," he blasted as he shifted gears. Nightmare-like fear gripped him while Amanda wrapped her arms across her middle. Was there no end to this?

AMANDA LOOKED IN the side mirror and didn't see the semi. Perhaps Bruce only thought he'd recognized it. She kept watch as they wound down the mountain, twisting and turning as they descended.

When the foothills came into sight, she saw him. Same ugly truck—blood, bugs, and guts plastered to the front grill. Dirty windshield. Impossible to make out the driver. He was gaining on them and they still had some tricky turns ahead, places where the road clung to the side of the mountain and made the threat of going over the edge and falling to their deaths real.

"Bruce, what are we going to do?"

"Out-maneuver the little creep," he spit out venomously.

Her hands hurt as she dug her nails into the front of the seat. Her breath came in ragged puffs, and she watched as spindly guardrails flew by. A plunge down the side was a small mistake away.

Heavenly Father, please, keep us safe.

The brief prayer was all she got out before Bruce cried out, "Hang on!"

With concentration born of desperation, Bruce steered the truck around the bend. The trailer wobbled behind them and ticked the posts one after the other as they passed.

The boss wasn't going to like the damage.

They made it into the foothills. Normally Bruce would have enjoyed the valleys and grasslands they passed through, but there was no time for that.

Now where was he supposed to turn? Was it two roads or three after the small white church? He tried to remember the instructions he'd gone over before they'd left the cabin. If he found the farm where he was to pick up the horses, they might be safe long enough to call the police.

The spire of the clapboard church was up on the right. The Creep was gaining. *Think. Remember. Quick! Two roads or three?* He tried to visualize the words the boss had written for him. It would be easier if he closed his eyes. *Better not try that.*

An old, green farm truck lumbered on the road in front of them. *Get out of the way!* He put his turn signal on to pass him just as a tanker came around the next corner toward them. *Oh, no!*

With no time to decide, he tramped the gas and whipped out into the oncoming lane, blowing past the green truck.

Amanda screamed. His ears rang with the high-pitched sound.

The oil truck blasted its horn. The noise jangled his nerves. He wanted to close his eyes and brace for the crash, but that was not an option. He steered, forcing his eyes to stay open. With a hair's breath to spare, he pulled back into his own lane and flew by the tanker. Air horn blasts from both vehicles rent the air as he tried to steady the truck and trailer.

Before he had his wits under control, he was at the third road past the church, and he slowed enough to make the corner, barely staying on the truck's four wheels. Tire tracks were ripped out of the grass and weeds when he failed to stay on the road until he finally maneuvered back onto the laneway.

Tears ran down Amanda's face.

"Sorry, Buttercup. I know this is crazy. Take some deep breaths. I'll keep you safe."

The last thing Bruce wanted to do was scare Amanda any more than she already was. He huffed out a sigh as the truck and trailer lumbered down the long, pot-holed driveway. White rail fences lined either side. His boss had told him it was a mile to the barn. Curious horses lifted their heads as they passed.

After five minutes, Amanda said, "Bruce, these horses are beautiful."

"Worth a cross-country ride?" He eyed her with a grin.

"Yes, look at that one," she said, pointing to a black stallion running the fence beside them.

"Hickory Acres is known for the best quarter horses in northern USA. Our cargo will be worth plenty of big money."

Nothing better go wrong.

"The first thing we'll do is pay for and load the horses then go inside and call the cops. We'll make a report and get the Creep outta our hair for good."

They pulled up beside a huge steel barn. They discovered it had a riding arena inside and stalls for many horses. At one end was a wellness clinic with a pool and all the exercise equipment needed to recondition a horse after surgery or a bad fall. A state-of-the-art facility.

Hickory Acres staff treated them like royalty. They fed them, helped them get the horses in the trailer, and let them use the boss's office to talk to the local sheriff and fill out a report on the Creep.

A sense of relief rode with him as they waved to the staff and headed down the bumpy lane to start the long trek home to New York. One of the staff had been fired so the owner offered them the phone he had used to communicate on the ranch. It still had a few minutes on it.

Bruce looked over at Amanda. An expression of contentment lit her face. Her hands lay relaxed in her lap. He pushed buttons on the radio until he found some classical music she would enjoy. *Fur Elise* by Beethoven came on.

It's scary that I recognize a classical song title and the composer. He patted her arm and she looked up at him, setting off a flutter in his chest.

This woman had really gotten to him. In a perfect world, he would marry her tomorrow, but because of the difference in their social backgrounds, he would have to content himself to store up memories to take with him during the long years ahead. He planned on spending the next four days kissing her as many times as she'd let him.

"Good grief!"

Amanda's words brought him up short. "What?"

"Is that him backed into that driveway up there?"

"Oh, come on. It can't be. How did the cops miss him?" Bruce tramped on the gas and sped past the idling truck. A shiver ran down his spine when the truck pulled out behind him, spewing black smoke from its stacks. The rumble of the powerful engine sent dread straight to his heart.

"Get the map out of the glove box, Mandy. We're gonna outfox this creep."

A knot in the middle of her forehead had transformed her face into a mask of fear. It hurt to think she was that upset. He had four very expensive horses in the back to worry about now. He couldn't race and take corners as he had before. He had to be mindful of how easily the trailer would tip and how the horses could bruise or break a leg if they became upset and began kicking.

An image of his boss handing him the truck's keys and wishing him a safe trip flashed through his thoughts.

"God be with us," he whispered.

AMANDA FOUND THE map and opened it, holding it up so Bruce could glance at it as he steered the truck back up into the mountains. He drove as fast as he dared with the horses in the back. The Creep taunted them by running up behind them then backing off when it looked like he would ram them, a sick game that he played all the way up the mountain.

"I'm so scared," she whispered.

"I wish I could get out of this truck and whip his butt."

"Please, don't do that. He'll run you over."

"I know. We need a plan. If we can just get down the other side of the mountain to the next town."

"Okay." Amanda's upset stomach settled a little as they barreled down the east side of the Rockies.

"Gee, what was I thinking?" Bruce's voice shattered the silence.

"What?"

"I have to get gas. Like, right now." He hit the steering wheel with the open palm of his hand. "Why am I so stupid?"

The gas gauge was close to empty. Amanda wiped at the sweat that popped out on her forehead. She had forgotten to keep track of the level, too.

If they ran out of gas before reaching the station, what would the Creep do? Careen into them? Drive them off the side of the mountain?

She wanted to cry. What would happen to Monica? Her sweet, fair-haired little angel.

White-knuckling it down the curving highway, they made it to the first gas station. The yellow sign had never looked so good. Amanda sat in the truck, listening for the sound of the approaching semi while Bruce went in to pay after he filled the tank.

Her door burst open and the Creep grabbed her arm. A long serrated knife in his right hand poked her ribs.

"Come with me and your friend won't get hurt."

Unable to think or feel, she climbed out of the truck and followed the Creep into the woods by the side of the lot. Her heart beat so fast she thought it would burst. It hurt to breathe by the time they travelled to where the semi stood chugging black smoke. The air stank with the smell of diesel fuel.

"What do you want?" she asked the slimy little man with the overgrown eyebrows. He hadn't shaved while he'd been chasing her, and he looked scruffier than the last time she had seen him at the ATM.

Without answering, he grabbed a length of rope with his free hand and tied her arms behind her back. She tripped, scraping her knee as he shoved her up into the big truck.

"Climb into the bunk," he barked. She remembered watching a documentary on TV once. The person interviewed said that once an abducted person was forced into a vehicle, they were a goner. She clawed, spit, and kicked until she felt the knife at her neck. No, she couldn't leave Monica motherless. She just couldn't.

Fetid breath assaulted her and she did what he asked. She held back the urge to vomit, closing her mouth. She lay on the bed behind the driver's seat. Body odor on the blankets made her stomach roll.

"I'm going to be sick," she whispered.

"Don't do it." He gave her a black look from the other side of the driver's seat.

Tears threatened to overwhelm her. She tried hard not to blink or they would spill down her cheeks. Her lips trembled with the effort to control her emotions.

He tied her ankles together and tethered the line so she couldn't escape. Her shoulder ached from the odd position she'd landed in.

Thoughts of Monica left without a mother tortured her. Alone to face the lonely childhood she herself had suffered. Left by herself with nannies or sent away to boarding school. She'd be brought up by uncaring grandparents too busy jet setting to pay attention to her little girl.

The tears streamed down her face. She had no way to wipe them away. When they came to a stop sign, Griffin noticed her tears and tenderly wiped them with his sleeve.

"Don't cry, little miss," he said in his goobery voice. "It's gonna be over soon." His coveralls had a name embroidered on the pocket. Griffin.

Fresh tears ran down her cheeks and splashed onto the gray army blanket. *Heavenly Father, please, help me.*

Through the windshield, she saw nothing but trees. They were in the midst of a forest. No one would hear if she screamed. The engine roared as the Creep drove out onto the highway. Nobody would hear her scream over the roar of the exhaust, and she knew that's why he hadn't gagged her.

"Why are you doing this? I don't even know you," she asked, thinking that if she engaged him in conversation maybe she'd find a way to reason with him.

"Oh, but I know who you are," he said in a high-pitched cackle.

"What do you want? Money?"

"You don't have enough cash to pay for what your husband did."

"My husband?" She sobbed. "He's dead."

"That was my brother, Harold's, doing."

She raised her head, trying to see him. "Your brother killed my husband?" He turned, nodded, and shot her a deadly stare. "Why? My husband was a doctor. He would never hurt anyone."

"Tell that to Harold when you see him. My mom went in for routine surgery and died."

"But, Griffin, Brad didn't kill her. He was trying to help her." She used the name on his coveralls, deciding to befriend him to defuse the situation.

"Who else was digging around inside her?"

Ugh, the man was so crass. What could she say to get him to let her go?

"What does your brother want with me?" she asked, trying to make sense of things.

"He says revenge is revenge, and killing the doctor wasn't enough. He said he'd kill someone dear to the doctor. Maybe that would make him feel better."

Killing her husband wasn't enough? His brother, whoever he was, was sick. She had to escape before Griffin took her to where ever Harold waited. Fear knotted in her throat as she tried to think.

Amanda rubbed at her wrists. They stung from the cord cutting into her flesh. She'd tried so hard to get loose, she'd lost the upper layers of skin. Raw and bleeding, she quit trying to escape.

If only Bruce could do something. Where was he? Hopefully, chasing them.

Maybe if she kept Griffin engaged in conversation she'd gain his sympathy. "How did you find us again?"

"No problem. I put another tracking device on the truck when you thought you were hiding at that cabin."

A cold shiver shot down her spine. "You were there in that terrible storm?"

"Harold said I had to."

It seemed the brother was in charge. "Griffin, you really don't want to do this, do you?"

"Sure I do. I do whatever my brother tells me."

A tanker going the opposite direction gave a blast on his air horn.

"Be careful. You're going too fast for these corners." She tried to keep her voice gentle, finding it hard to stay calm.

The semi rounded a corner, leaning too far to the left.

Amanda slid.

Yelled.

Hit the floor.

Hard.

Her head bounced off the seat in front of her. Everything went black.

BRUCE RACED AFTER the speeding truck. How did the Creep get Amanda? He was only in the gas station a couple of minutes. If only his boss's credit card had gone through right away, this wouldn't have happened. The system had been busy and it had taken a few tries for the attendant to get the transaction to take.

Bruce's head pounded. He could not let them get away. He'd have no way to find Amanda once they left the mountains. He tried the Hickory Acres cell phone, but of course no signal.

His breathing came in ragged gasps as he chased them, taking corners far too fast as he raced after the semi. He had to catch the Creep before he had time to hurt Amanda. He passed cars on corners and blasted by trucks in his quest to keep the dirty semi with its precious cargo in sight.

He loved her.

The realization hit with sudden ferocity. Yes, he did. He swallowed hard.

Why try to deny it? They could never be together. That was a given, but it didn't change the fact that when he went back to the ranch and she went home to her daughter, he would still be in love with her.

Probably love her until the day he died.

Please, God, help me save her so she can be with Monica.

The sound of metal hitting wood met him as he rounded a corner.

Smoke billowed up from the trees a mile ahead.

Bile rose in Bruce's throat.

Oh, please, Lord, let them still be alive.

He turned the final bend to see flames and black smoke engulfing the semi's engine. The truck had left the road and plowed a path into the forest. It had knocked down trees until finally coming to rest against a big pine tree. Steam rose at the front grill of the semi. He scanned for survivors, but no one stood outside the truck.

His truck was still rolling when he jammed it into park and sprinted down the embankment. Following the path of the big rig's tire tracks, he raced, jumping over fallen pines and mountain ash trunks. Brambles scratched his legs, slowing him, and he almost tripped when his foot caught in a twisted vine.

The Creep was in the cab, terror in his eyes, trying to free Amanda from the tether he had earlier tied her feet up with so she couldn't escape.

Bruce yelled, "Amanda." He wrenched open the passenger door. His vision blurry at first, he struggled to clear it. The creep suddenly slumped against the steering wheel and looked to be losing consciousness. He appeared to be pinned there.

Bruce swiped at the moisture in his eyes. When his vision cleared, he saw Amanda lying on the floor behind the front seats.

Heat built in the cab as Bruce worked to free the cord that held her in place. His fingers pulled at the knots. It was taking forever. A wall of flames licked at the windshield, seeping out from under the hood. He dug harder at the knots that refused to slip over the knob of the gearshift. The cab was filling with smoke.

Cuss words were on the edge of his tongue. Words he hadn't used in a very long time.

"Please, Lord, help me," he uttered instead. The heat was unbearable, he would have to give up soon. The fuel tank could rupture at any moment. With one last try, the corded knots finally gave way.

Amanda's eyelids fluttered as he scooped her up and pulled her out. He held her against him—the most precious bundle he had ever held.

He carried her out into the trees and set her down in the leaves and pine needles by a tree. She appeared lifeless, so he grabbed her wrist and felt for a pulse. A weak, thready rhythm beat beneath his fingers.

"Mandy." He shook her and she groaned. "It's okay, Buttercup. I've got you."

She started coming around. Her eyes grew big as saucers when she finally became oriented. He had his back to the truck when he noticed her expression change.

"Fire." It came out as a whisper, putting all his senses on alert. "Where's Griffin?"

"Who?"

"The Creep. His name is Griffin. We have to save him. The truck's on fire."

Smoke billowed in great clouds from under the hood of the tanker and the flames he'd seen earlier were now making their way to the fuel tank.

AMANDA SCRAMBLED TO her feet, tripped, and stumbled. Before she could run back to the semi, Bruce pulled her aside.

"Wait, I'll get him. You stay back." Bruce jumped into the passenger side of the truck and yanked on Griffin's slumped body. He grabbed him under the arms and pulled hard, but there was little movement.

Seeing he was wedged between his seat and the dashboard, Amanda sprinted to the driver's door. Pain shot through her arm as she struggled to open it. Her right hip stung as she leapt onto the running board. Her head was hazy as she tried to reason out what to do.

Smoke filled the cab now and the smell of burning rubber rose from under the dash. They had to get him out. Fast.

"Griffin, Griffin," she called.

"Push his legs toward me." Bruce yanked at his clothes to free him.

After she gave his legs a final shove toward Bruce, she lifted on the steering column with all her strength. Finally, Bruce freed him and carried him fireman-style to the half-ton idling on the side of the highway. She stumbled behind them, climbing up the embankment with great difficulty. She scraped her knees when she fell in the underbrush a couple of times, but got right up and kept going.

A siren wailed in the distance as Amanda joined Bruce. He had laid Griffin in the gravel and talked to him in an assertive voice. Had he become conscious? She couldn't tell. She wanted to hear what Bruce said, but she was too exhausted. She slumped to the ground and leaned against the tire of the truck.

The police finally arrived and took over. After filling them in on the accident, Bruce crawled to her side. His warmth was comforting.

"Mandy, your head's bleeding."

She reached up, pulled her hand out of her hair, saw the blood, and everything went black.

CHAPTER TWENTY-TWO

THE POLICE RECOGNIZED Griffin's truck from the APB report and took him to the patrol car after the ambulance attendants had brought him out of his unconscious state and checked him over for injuries.

An officer kindly offered to take care of the horses, telling Bruce a nearby rancher would be willing to board them until he was able to claim them. Then Bruce climbed into the ambulance where Amanda was strapped to a gurney and covered in a bright silver blanket. The police officer gave him a thumbs-up and the attendant closed the doors. The siren wailed and gravel crunched beneath the tires as they sped off.

It wasn't long before Bruce's head began pounding again, made worse by the noise and stress. Amanda's eyes fluttered open. She appeared more alert, and she nodded in answer to the attendant's questions.

Bruce clung to her hand and refused to release it. The EMT took blood pressure readings on the other arm. Through the racket and confusion in his head, Bruce asked, "Are you all right?"

"Yes. I'm just shook up. I'll be fine."

She would be sore tomorrow, he thought

Tomorrow.

Tomorrow, her parents would come to take her home and he wouldn't see her again. A boulder landed in his stomach and stayed there. Sorrow seized him in a vise-like grip and he rubbed at his chest. How would he face saying good-bye to her?

HE'D SPENT THE night in a hotel near the hospital. The off-duty police officer brought the half-ton and horses to him at eight the next morning. He left them parked in the shade by a cool fountain near the hospital. It was nine now, and he'd been sitting in the ugly hospital waiting room for what seemed like hours. Why weren't they letting him visit Amanda?

"Amanda's parents have been notified and are returning to the country. Her mother will fly in, rent a car, and take her home."

"What's happening with the driver?" Bruce asked.

"Griffin will remain in custody. They expect him to make a full recovery in the prison ward in University Hospital. His brother, Harold, was shot when they went to arrest him."

Griffin had told the officers that he'd acted under his brother's orders. The revenge had to do with Amanda's husband operating on their mother who had died during surgery. The detectives suspected that the brother and Griffin killed Amanda's husband, Brad, blaming him because their mother hadn't come through the surgery. In their sick minds, they wanted further revenge by kidnapping Amanda and torturing her until they felt they had justice.

"Wow, they're a couple of sick people."

"I understand they had a violent upbringing with a mentally ill mother and abusive father."

It was a strange tale, but Bruce didn't really care as long as the danger was over.

A nurse came out of Amanda's room down the hall with an arm full of dirty linen. Bruce walked to meet her. "She's ready for visitors now."

"Thanks."

Heart pounding, he opened the door. Amanda sat in the bed, propped up with pillows. She looked like she'd been in a terrible fight. She had a fat lip and the side of her face was bruised where she'd landed between the seats in the crash. She smiled a lopsided grin when she spied him in the doorway. The love he held for this woman expanded his chest, and he had to stop halfway to her and catch his breath.

If only she was some poor farmer's daughter, he'd marry her and make a home for her and Monica.

He crossed the room and she was in his arms. The scent of strawberry shampoo and liniment lingered in the air. She was crying. He felt her tears against his cheek. He inched back and she kissed him, kissed him like a woman in love. Kissed him with all the love a woman can give a man. At first, he was stunned. Then he kissed her back.

"Mandy," he whispered.

Any minute her parents would arrive and he'd have to say good-bye forever. He'd allow himself these few stolen moments. Moments he would remember for the rest of his life.

He threaded his fingers through her silky hair, something he'd longed to do for a while. He deepened the kiss, going somewhere he'd never been with any other woman. Ecstasy.

"Ha…hem." A female voice ended the silence in the room and he pulled away.

Amanda didn't react. Apparently, she hadn't heard the visitor. She followed him, leaning forward, arms outstretched, seeking another kiss.

A woman in a blue business suit stood inside the doorway. Her cold frown drilled into Bruce, making him shudder. The stranger was correct. He had no right to be kissing Amanda.

AMANDA RECOVERED FROM the kiss, red-faced when she recognized her mother in the doorway. Outward shows of affection were frowned upon in her family. Her cheeks burned, because she'd been caught reaching for Bruce, her lips pursed for another kiss. Dying of embarrassment, she wanted to hide. She'd known she would have to face the reality of her life, but seeing her mother wasn't making it easy. Her time with Bruce had wrapped her in a happy cocoon where he kept her safe.

"Where is Monica, Mother?"

"Aren't you glad to see me?" She crossed the room and, turning her back, she fussed with the flowers she'd brought, arranging them on the window ledge.

"Of course, I'm happy to see you, Mum." She stared at the doorway, hoping Monica would appear. "Did you bring Monica?"

Her mother turned. "No. I did not bring Monica." Looking Bruce up and down, she added, "And it's a good thing I didn't."

Did she have to be so rude?

"Mother, this is Bruce Palmer." Bruce had taken off his Stetson and stood with it in front of him. Her mother offered Bruce a stiff hand to shake. "Bruce saved me from the man who captured me."

That had no effect. Her mother turned her back on him and played with a box of facial tissues on the table beside the bed.

"I better go," Bruce said, backing away.

"Yes, well. Good-bye," Mrs. Vanderbilt snapped.

"No. Please, don't go." Amanda fumbled with the rail, trying to push it down.

"It's best if I do." His gaze drilled into her mother's back. Then Bruce turned and walked out.

Amanda managed to push the rail down and ran barefoot into the hall. Her feet slapped the tile as she chased Bruce. With her back to the wall to hide the open back of her hospital gown, she grabbed his sleeve.

"Bruce, you can't just go like this." She took a breath. "I need to thank you."

"No thanks needed, Buttercup." His adorable blue eyes looked down at her.

"But you saved me and risked your life. And you were so good to me when we were on the road. I owe you."

"No, you don't." He huffed out a long breath. "This has to end here, Amanda. We both knew it would come to this. Now, please, don't make it any harder." The pleading in his eyes caused her to lose her grip on his arm.

"I love you," she whispered.

"I know," he said. Then he turned and walked away.

How can he just walk away? Doesn't he love me, too?

He does. I know he does!

She raced back to her hospital room and the sanctuary of her bed. Burrowing under the covers, she let the tears flow. The sorrow of a lifetime without him poured out on to her pillow.

A DEEP, ALL-CONSUMING ache settled in her midsection as Amanda peered out the passenger window of her mother's Mercedes, willing the ache to subside. The doctor swore it was emotional pain. Mother was convinced it was physical—from her 'ordeal,' as she called it.

She tried not to think about Bruce. He'd made it clear they had no future together.

Everyday something would remind her of him. A truck pulling a horse trailer. What was someone doing pulling a horse trailer in the middle of New York? Really!

A man in a cowboy hat. Buttercups along the side of a laneway.

Why had she never noticed these things before?

SHE SPENT HOURS by the pool in the back yard while Monica played in the sandbox or splashed in the shallow end with her water wings.

Amanda thought about what she wanted to do with her life. So far, she'd lived a useless existence. Endless parties and shopping. She needed to find a purpose. When it came right down to it, she really wanted to share her life with Bruce. To be with Bruce and Monica and spend time together—the three of them.

She knew Bruce wouldn't be comfortable in the city. Her mother had made that abundantly clear. This was the only life she'd ever known.

The farm in Indian Head called to her. She had loved it there. Though busy with activity, somehow it was tranquil, too. She often thought about the corral with the horses. The ride she'd taken with Bruce. The way she felt while there. At home somehow. At peace within herself.

It was easy to picture Monica being there. She'd love it, too. She'd make friends with the local children, but she'd really love Kohkom, making cookies and bannock while listening to Kohkom's stories.

One day, out of boredom, Amanda gave the cook the afternoon off, took over the kitchen and made bannock with Monica.

"The first time I made this, we made it outside over an open fire." Monica's eyes grew wide as Amanda kneaded the dough. "But we'll make it in the oven today."

She placed the bannock into the oven with a sigh, hoping that, when they ate it, some of the ache in her heart would subside.

Maybe when she tasted it she would feel a little closer to Bruce, her cowboy.

UNLOADING THE HORSES was a bittersweet victory for Bruce. He'd come so close to losing them on the mountain, yet abandoning them to concentrate on keeping Amanda safe had been a real temptation. When he watched them romp in the field, it gave him a sense of pride in a job accomplished.

Well, he had fences to check and mend.

He finished cinching his saddle, checked his gear, mounted Stardust, and headed south along the barbed wire.

This was where he belonged, in a saddle on a ranch, doing the work he loved most. Now if he could just pray hard enough to restore Matt to health, he'd have one less thing to fret about. But worry was a knot in his gut as he watched for breaks in the wire.

What would become of the farm and Kohkom if Matt didn't get better? Nola was too busy with her career in town to manage the ranch. Kohkom was slowing down a little more every year. In her younger days, she would have taken over, but not now. The technological advancement in equipment alone was an ongoing learning curve.

He stopped at the spot where the fence was broken and lay in the grass. Moose again. They were a rancher's worst enemy when it came to barbed wire. A deer would jump over a cattle fence, but moose plowed right through, leaving hours of work repairing the damage.

Bruce huffed out a sigh as he stepped down to access the hole this one had left. He scanned the area for escaped cows and that's when he saw buttercups by a stream.

A vision of Amanda came unbidden. His Buttercup in her yellow top. A lump always formed when he thought of her, and he couldn't stop thinking about her.

Missing her.

How was she? She'd be happy to be home with Monica. That woman loved her child. Did she suffer nightmares from her ordeal with the Creep?

As he strung the wire, he wished he'd met Monica. When he thought about her, she was a fuzzy image. He would have liked to have seen her once, so when he prayed for her and her mom, like he did now, he'd have a clearer picture of Amanda's angel.

He kicked at the old fencepost. Rotten. It needed to be replaced. His thoughts needed to be replaced. He needed to stick to reality and forget about her.

At the end of the day, he rode into the yard. Tired, but satisfied after a productive day's work, looking forward to a long, hot shower and a meal with the men. Curly would have roast beef or stew ready as the ranch hands came in off the range.

Bruce was in the barn removing Stardust's saddle when his boss walked in.

"I have a message for you." The no-nonsense tone in his voice alerted Bruce something was wrong.

"What is it?" His gut twisted.

"Your sister-in-law called. Matt's in a bad way. They need you to go home to Canada right away." Hank patted his shoulder. "Go, son. We'll be fine here."

All the fear he'd been holding at bay crashed down on him, knotting his stomach.

"Matt, hold on," he whispered as he strode from the barn.

CHAPTER TWENTY-THREE

MATT WAS IN the hospital in Regina, the nearest big center to his family's farm. Bruce took a flight through Toronto to get there the fastest way possible. Nola met him at the Regina airport. As he held her in a hug, he discovered she'd lost weight. When he released her, he noticed the lines of stress and grief on her face. His heart ached and he gave her another embrace.

His arm around her shoulders, they walked to the baggage claim. "You okay, Nola?"

"Yah." He felt her nod against his shoulder.

"How is Kohkom holding up?"

"You know her. She's binding the rest of us together."

"I know." After giving her shoulder a squeeze, he picked up his bag, and they headed to the parking lot. "And Matt?" he asked as they settled into Nola's car.

She shook her head. "He's weary. It's been a long struggle and the chemo has stopped working. If he isn't going to win the fight, then he's ready to go. He's just waiting to see you."

"Thank goodness for our faith."

As Nola drove them through city traffic to the hospital, Bruce thought about salvation and the reassurance of a home in heaven. In Sunday school, he'd learned God had a mansion waiting for Matt in Heaven—for everyone who surrendered their lives to Him. A place where there was no more sorrow or pain. The thought gave him comfort. Knowing Matt would be in a better place made it easier to release Matt to what now seemed inevitable.

He followed Nola into the hospital room and gasped when he saw his brother. While she was kissing Matt, Bruce took a moment to recover from the shock. Matt was a pasty gray. His cheeks were sunken, and his eyes had lost their luster. The monitors beeped and whirred—reassuring and frightening at the same time.

This was the boy he used to play with, get in trouble with, and sleep in the same bed with. It hurt to breathe, his throat on fire with unshed tears. Letting Matt go was going to be the hardest thing he'd ever done.

When Nola stepped aside, he tried to shake his brother's hand. Matt was having none of that. Instead, he pulled him into a bear hug. The tears flowed then. There was no holding them back.

His brother was dying.

Oh, Matt.

Kohkom came in with a carafe of coffee for all of them, and they visited for an hour until Matt fell asleep.

Later, as they walked through the dark parking lot, Bruce said, "I had no idea he would go downhill so fast."

Nola hit the remote and the car beeped. "He knows it's time, and he's ready to go."

"It won't be long now," Kohkom said as Bruce helped her into the passenger seat.

"We need to talk, Bruce," Nola spoke when Bruce settled into the back seat. "The three of us, when we get home."

"Okay." The pain in his heart increased as they drove to Indian Head.

THEY SAT IN the living room in his grandmother's comfortable chairs. Kohkom made a pot of tea. Bruce blew on his and sipped at it, waiting for someone to speak.

"We need you here now, Bruce," Kohkom spoke in her direct way.

"Of course. I'll be here 'til after the funeral."

"Now you live here," Kohkom said, drilling him with her gaze before looking away.

Nola spoke, "What she means, Bruce, is that you need to come home and run the ranch."

They must be kidding. The farm went to Matt. It wasn't rightly his. It should be Nola's.

"I have a job." He couldn't leave his boss in the lurch, could he?

"You have a duty here," Kohkom spoke in her matter of fact way.

Bruce ground his jaw shut and shook his head.

"She means the property passes to you now, Bruce." Nola gave him some legal-looking papers. "When you read it, it states the ranch belongs to you upon Matt's passing with the stipulation that Kohkom and I can live here if we wish."

Bruce took a deep breath. This meant he would leave his current job for real and move back to Canada, something he hadn't considered doing. To own the farm at Indian Head would be a wonderful thing, but he would be farther from Amanda.

What did that matter? She was out of his life anyway. That stopped him. Deep in his heart, she still mattered. He longed for her in his waking moments and in his dreams at night, too.

Nola tapped his shoulder. "What are you thinking?" she asked.

He came away from his thoughts. "I guess I'm thinking I need to give my boss my notice."

Kohkom gave a sigh of relief and mumbled something in Cree. She smiled and Bruce did, too. He'd done the right thing.

BRUCE'S BOSS WAS good about him leaving. "I'm sad to see you go, Palmer, but glad you have your own place now. You'll do well."

They exchanged a heartfelt hug then Bruce got into his dusty blue pickup loaded with his belongings. He drove away from Sheffield Farms for the last time, pulling a rented horse trailer with Stardust in tow.

"Going home," he whispered. "God, I pray I've made the right decision. Please, be with me."

As he left New York State, his heart was heavy—Amanda left behind. It wouldn't be an easy thing to do, but he had to stop wishing.

LIVING AT INDIAN Head again was like coming back to his childhood. Walking by the dugout pond to check the cattle reminded Bruce of hot summer days, swimming with his brother and friends from the reserve.

One of the kids had almost drowned in the deep water. He'd been too embarrassed to admit he didn't know how to swim. Bruce had saved him. The children had treated Bruce like a hero that day. All he remembered was wishing the boy had trusted him with his secret before he'd jumped in.

They'd spent the following weeks making sure all of them could swim well enough so that nothing like that happened again. He'd had nightmares for a long time after, of the boy almost dying and taking Bruce under, too, as the kid tried to climb on his back in the deep water.

He found it difficult to pass by the place between Indian Head and Regina where his mom and dad had died in the accident. They had been snowmobiling after dark and hadn't noticed the open water. The people with them had gone to shore and found branches to try to save them, but they had slipped under the ice and were gone.

When he walked into the shed behind the house for the first time, he stopped. The memory of kissing Amanda there brought back the smells and sounds of that night. He took a deep breath and went to the corner where the shovel lay, trying to stop the soft, inescapable memory of Amanda in his arms in the dark, kissing him back.

If only. If only they were different people.

More memories assaulted him. Amanda wearing her yellow top. Amanda in the bunk of the camper. Amanda laughing at something he said. Amanda smiling at him in the seat next to him in the truck. Would he ever stop thinking of her? Unfortunately, his sorrow didn't go unnoticed.

Yesterday, Nola had cornered him in the car on the way to the hospital. "What's wrong, Bruce? I don't ever remember you so preoccupied." She tapped his arm. "Is it Matt?"

How could he tell her it wasn't his brother's eminent death that had him so flummoxed? It was a girl with curly, golden hair and a smile that lit up his soul. The same girl who, like the stars, was beyond his reach.

CHAPTER TWENTY-FOUR

AMANDA SAT WITH Monica, helping her solve a toddler puzzle of three little kittens playing with a ball of yarn. They were in the middle of the living room floor on the freshly vacuumed carpet. Monica's little head bent over it in concentration, reciting the alphabet song as she placed the pieces one after another.

"Look, Momma, I made the orange cat picture."

"Yes, sweetheart. You did." She patted her blonde curls. "You're so good at this."

Sophia approached with the phone in hand. "A call for you, miss."

Amanda hadn't heard it ring. Eyes raised to the maid's face, Amanda mouthed, "who?"

She answered with her hand over the mouthpiece so the caller wouldn't hear. "Long distance. She didn't give her name."

Amanda stood up and took a long breath, steeling herself for a session with someone selling something.

"Hello?"

"Amanda, this is Nola Palmer."

Amanda's heart tapped a rapid rhythm. "Oh, Nola, hi." Relief, then dread, settled in her stomach.

"I'm calling with sad news. Matt passed away yesterday. I was hoping you would come for the funeral on Friday afternoon at three and stay for the weekend."

She recognized the sadness in Nola's voice. It tore at her heart. "Yes, of course I'll come."

"Good. We have the spare bedroom here and, if you'd like, bring the daughter that Bruce is always talking about. She can stay here with all the cousins during the funeral. The teens will be watching the little ones."

"Okay, I'll try to arrange that. Nola, I'm so sorry."

There was a pause before Nola spoke again. "Well, we knew the day would come." Nola dissolved into tears. Small muffled sobs broke the silence.

"I'll fly into Regina on Friday. Don't worry about picking me up at the airport. I'll rent a car."

"All right." Nola sobbed and said, "Bye for now."

Amanda sat down in her dad's recliner. Her strength was suddenly gone, like the wind out of a sail. As she listened to her own breathing, she wondered what it would be like to see Bruce again. Was it wise to go? It'd been months since she'd seen him. She was trying hard to forget him, but it was almost impossible.

She should have refused Nola's invitation. Let sleeping dogs lie. Could she see him after all this time and not stir up the old feelings she'd tamped down? And what of Monica?

Should she take Monica? She would love Kohkom, Nola, and all the farm animals. It'd be a treat to let her see the beauty of the flat, open prairie that stretched for miles.

She might regret it, but she would go and take Monica with her. She'd check flight schedules as soon as she helped Monica pack up her puzzle.

AMANDA AND MONICA landed in Regina late in the morning on Friday, rented a car, and drove straight to Indian Head. Monica bounced in her car seat in the back, excited and happy to be on an adventure with her mom. Amanda hoped all would go well.

When they turned into the driveway at the Palmer's farm, Amanda took deep breaths. Her hands ached when she took them from the steering wheel.

Please, God, be with me.

Something life-changing had happened to her that day in the Indian Head church with Bruce. God's strength was her first thought. He was her focus now, since she'd realized she could have a personal relationship with Him. She prayed every day now and was attending a small church with believers the same as those back in Indian Head.

The yard had a couple of extra vehicles in it that she didn't recognize. Relatives in for the funeral, she assumed.

She unbuckled Monica from her seat as the farm dogs came to greet them, a border collie and a chocolate lab. She set Monica on the ground and the dogs waited to be petted. Amanda had forgotten how well-behaved they were, trained by Matt to sit when visitors dropped by.

A door banged. When Amanda looked up, Bruce stood on the porch. Tears instantly moistened her eyes. Her chest ached as he came down the steps toward her—thinner, wearing blue jeans and a sky-blue shirt. A welcoming smile lit his face.

She hesitated for only a second, long enough to make sure Monica made friends with the dogs. Then her shaking legs carried her across the hard ground and into Bruce's arms. She felt his tears on her cheek as his arms swallowed her up in a hug, whispering, "Buttercup."

"My cowboy," she said, her heart singing with joy.

Oh, she might regret coming, but, at that moment, she didn't care.

BRUCE REVELED IN Amanda's scent. He held her tight to him. How could he have tried to tell himself he didn't really love her? She was everything, his sunshine, his air, his Buttercup.

The hug ended with a bittersweet feeling. Then he spotted her.

Monica.

The cutest little cherub he'd ever seen, on her knees in the dirt, petting the dogs. She looked up and lifted her arms to be picked up. He glanced at Amanda for permission and she nodded. Nothing prepared him for the thud of his heart as he hoisted the pretty little girl into his arms. She sat against his chest as if she belonged there.

"Hi, I'm Monica." Then she smiled a smile that was uniquely hers as she played with the brim of his Stetson.

He caught Amanda's proud gaze and smiled. All the love he had in the world beamed down on these two girls. He had to have them in his life. There had to be a way.

Amanda reddened and looked away. Had she read his mind?

He wrapped an arm around Amanda's shoulders. With Monica still in his other arm, he steered them into his home.

Bruce introduced Amanda to the people she didn't know. She gave Nola a hug and accepted a seat at the table. All gazes fell on the wee girl in his arms as Bruce presented Monica to everyone, and when he came to Kohkom, Monica reached out to go to her. He heard Amanda's breath catch as her little girl sat in Kohkom's lap and helped cut out the cookies she was making.

How was it possible the love of his life was finally here in his kitchen?

IN THE AFTERNOON before the funeral, Nola introduced Amanda to Carrie, the babysitter. She was Nola and Matt's niece, Nola's sister's daughter, who'd come home from college specifically to be with family during this sad time. Carrie took Monica by the hand and led her into the living room where three children played on the rug with several toys. Amanda watched Monica settle in and help a boy build a tower with colored blocks.

After bringing her a cup of coffee, Bruce excused himself and went to change for the funeral.

When it was time to go, Amanda was still apprehensive about leaving Monica. "Are you okay staying here with Carrie for a while? Mommy will be back soon."

She barely looked up as she nodded "yes" and continued to play with a boy who looked to be about two years older. Amanda had observed them from the other room as they'd played for hours. He seemed patient and gentle while encouraging Monica to do a good job with the blocks.

Bruce whispered in her ear as they left, "Carrie will keep an eye on them. Don't worry."

Amanda smiled as Bruce escorted her to his truck. She prayed for his family while Bruce drove to the Band offices at File Hill. The building was a two-story, modern brick at one end and, at the other, a stylized teepee. The teepee was much like a town council's chambers inside.

CHAPTER TWENTY-FIVE

BRUCE PULLED INTO the parking lot. Amanda looked down at her hands in her lap. Clasped tight, the knuckles had turned white. She shook them as she stepped out of the car. Bruce ushered them inside.

"We'll be in the gymnasium today. It's the only room that will hold all of us," he whispered, holding the door for her.

She smiled, loving his attentiveness, so happy to be with him again.

The casket sat on the opposite side of the room. Five chairs were behind it, close to the wall. The far gym door stood open—someone tended a fire outside. The orange flames flickered and smoke rose into the air. For her, it was a strange sight at a funeral.

Bruce took her to a room in the Band offices where the family assembled. Kohkom sat in a chair on her right and reached for her hand. A warm sensation spread through her chest. Kohkom had chosen to draw strength from her. She gave the elderly woman a warm glance and squeezed her hand. Bruce's grandmother gave a tiny smile in return.

Bruce sat beside Nola with his arm around her. He seemed to be whispering comforting words to her in Cree. Nola's mother sat on the other side, offering tissues. Nola looked so broken. Her face was lined with grief, her eyes puffy and swollen. Her shoulders slumped in defeat. Tears gathered in Amanda's eyes and she brushed them away. She needed to stay strong for them.

Time passed quickly, and soon an elder stood in the doorway beckoning them to come.

One at a time, Bruce and Kohkom led them in a brief prayer and then they proceeded into the gym. Everyone stood silent as they went to the chairs on the right side of the casket. Nola slumped into a chair, as if her legs could no longer support her. Amanda's heart broke for her. Bruce took the seat beside Amanda. Love like a river swelled in her chest for this man who was so bereft. She longed to comfort him.

An elder stood by the casket and the room came to a hush.

"We have decided to have an all-Cree funeral. We do this so that Matthew—Soaring Eagle—will have a safe journey. We don't want to do anything wrong. I apologize to the others who are here. We do not want to offend anyone, but we will be speaking in Cree."

He proceeded to perform the ceremony in Cree, and Amanda wished with all her heart that she understood the language. The odor of smoke and burning sweet grass entered the room. A man carried what looked like a frying pan glowing with coals from the outside fire. He held the pan in one hand and an eagle feather in the other. He gently waved the eagle feather, sending the smoke from the sweet grass over Matt's body. He walked around the casket, covering the body with the smoke.

Then he stood in front of the elder who looked as if he washed himself in the smoke. Cupping his hands, he held them over the pan and gathered smoke three times, pulling it over his head. Then he pulled it over his chest three times. It was as if he purified himself.

He spoke to the crowd in Cree for several minutes, then someone else spoke. Each person who talked used the smoke in the same way. There were only a couple of people who spoke English, and when they did, it was a relief to understand what was happening. Amanda finally felt she was participating.

After everyone who wanted to speak had a turn, the elder asked the family to stand. Drummers sat on the other side of the casket and they began to chant and drum. Amanda wondered if they chanted words or if the sound was guttural, sacred sounds. Her pulse sped up and a thrill travelled down her spine. Primitive, she thought, and stood in awe. The only other time she'd come across this was at the sound of bagpipes.

The room vibrated with the sound of the drums, and physical vibrations of the drumming, stirring something primal within her. A sensation rarely ever felt. A core experience.

Wondering how to proceed, she watched as the family began to file past the coffin. Some kissed the deceased, others laid a hand on his chest. One of the elders who'd spoken in English spoke about Matt's journey, so she placed her hand on his chest and wished him well on his journey.

After the family passed the body, paying their respect, they took their seats in the front row again. Bruce hugged each person who had been in the line ahead of him, then took his place at the end of the row. Amanda followed him. The people had lined up behind them, filing past first the coffin and then past the mourners and offered condolences. Many cried openly.

She learned that it was the Native way to bury their dead before sundown, so they proceeded to the gravesite and buried Matt with more tears and open sadness.

A feast had been prepared in their absence. Tables covered with white linens and laden with food filled the gym. Except for the wild meat, the buffet offered to the guests was the same as what she was used to seeing at the funerals she'd attended.

When they arrived home, everyone was tired. All the children were sleeping in the living room. Monica was at one end of the couch, and a cousin named Sofie was at the opposite end. The rest were in sleeping bags spread out on the rug.

Kohkom had assigned the single bed in the sewing room to Amanda. A partially made quilt was on the table and Amanda admired it. It was pieced together in various shades of burgundy—a beautiful work of art, possibly an heirloom.

A ROOSTER CROWING woke Amanda with a start. She had two days to spend with Bruce. She washed and dressed in a hurry, not wanting to waste a moment.

Kohkom stood at the stove, frying pancakes for everyone. Bruce was making coffee for the adults. Carrie had the kids up and putting their sleeping bags and gear by the back door.

Monica came and crawled up into Amanda's lap, sleepy eyed, but smiling.

"Did you sleep well, sweetie?"

Monica nodded. "Sofie wants to know if I can go to her house today."

Bruce turned and gave her a nod. "Sofie is Nola's niece. Nola's sister will keep her safe."

It was hard to let Monica go with strangers, but she trusted Bruce's judgment. After what they'd been through together, how he'd been so good and kind to her, she couldn't imagine him allowing anything to happen to her child.

The adults took their coffee into the living room while Kohkom and Carrie fed the children. Then Carrie took the kids outside while the grownups ate in the kitchen. Excited to be with their cousins, they were too wild to play inside. Nola hadn't come down yet. Amanda assumed they were letting her sleep in after her long, emotional day yesterday.

She said a silent prayer for Nola's recovery after such a tragic loss. Matt was far too young to be taken home to Heaven.

Kohkom left to go upstairs to change, so Bruce gathered the plates and filled the sink with soapy water. Lemon-scented detergent drifted to Amanda where she sat finishing her second cup of coffee.

Bruce at the sink doing dishes reminded her of their days together in the trailer. A warm, fuzzy feeling invaded her chest as she rose and picked up a tea towel to help dry. While standing beside him, a heart-felt longing enveloped her.

This is just a physical sensation, she told herself. *You can't base your future on physical attraction.* She was making progress, talking herself out of her feelings, until he turned his smile on her.

Oh, my!

She trembled with the impact.

How was she ever going to go home and get over him? Coming here was a big mistake. Well, if she had to say good-bye, then she would just make as many good memories as possible while she was here.

BRUCE LOOKED DOWN into Amanda's eyes. She was so beautiful. So perfect.

"How would you like to take a drive with me?" he asked as he pulled the plug to drain the dishwater.

She hesitated as she dried the last glass. For a moment, he thought she would refuse. Then she looked up and said, "Sure."

After releasing the breath he'd been holding, he said, "I'll meet you at the truck in ten minutes."

She left to get her purse and freshen up while he made up a quick lunch to take with them.

She was waiting by the pickup when he carried the bag with sandwiches, apples, and drinks out and placed them in the cab. She'd changed into the yellow top, the one purchased on their trip—the exact color of buttercups. She would always be buttercup to him, even if she wasn't in his life.

They buckled into their seats, and soon he headed out along the highway to Fort Qu'Appelle. He planned to go to a place on the water a mile or two from town.

He took her to a secluded place in the valley carved out long ago by an ancient waterway. The spot had plenty of trees and a grassy bank. Peaceful bird songs greeted them as Bruce spread the blanket under a poplar tree. He needed to talk to Amanda and find out if there was any chance he could have a future with her.

He opened the bag and passed a sandwich and a can of juice to her. The smile she gave him sent his pulse racing.

Please, God, help me.

He'd been thinking of her night and day and imagined making a life together with her on the ranch. Was it possible she might consider changing her whole life for him? It was asking a lot of her to give up the privileged life she lived, but if she loved him half as much as he loved her, then he stood a chance.

She sat, watching him with an expectant expression on her face.

Oh, yes, grace.

He bowed his head and spoke from the heart. "Heavenly Father, I thank You for the opportunity to have this meal and this time alone with Amanda. May You please bless our time together. May Your will be done, as always. I pray in the name of Jesus, because I love You, Lord. Amen."

Amanda's eyes were moist when she lifted her head, and his pulse kicked up a notch. This woman was so precious. He wanted to kiss her so bad. Did he dare? The look she gave him made him think that she wanted that, too. But could he handle it if she rejected him?

They finished their sandwiches and he passed an apple to her. She took delicate little bites. Oh, if only he'd thought of packing finger foods he could feed her. Oh, boy, now his thoughts were running away on him.

Focus, Palmer. This has to go just right.

"How have you been since you returned to New York?" he asked. "Have you had problems with nightmares?"

"I was afraid to sleep for a while when I first got home. The dreams were very intense. But they aren't quite so bad now. They don't come as often. Maybe once a week."

"Good. I wondered how you coped with everything you went through with the Creep."

She gave a hint of a smile. "You're still calling him that?"

"Yeah." He shrugged.

"I feel sorry for Griffin. He was a pawn in his brother's schemes. Too afraid to stand up for himself." She sighed.

"Right, I read in the paper his brother was a psychopath from an early age. Mean to animals, Griffin, and to other kids."

"Yes, at least Griffin showed remorse. His brother certainly didn't." Amanda twirled a piece of grass in her fingers. "Let's change the subject."

He finished eating, packed the apple cores and sandwich wrappers away, and then said, "Monica seems to fit in here. My grandmother certainly took to her."

"Yes, it's wonderful. She really loves the farm."

Amanda went on to describe an incident that involved the cats in the barn. Bruce had trouble concentrating on the story as Amanda occupied his thoughts.

He'd brought her on the picnic with the intention of finding out if she'd ever entertained the idea of living on the farm with him. He loved her so much. She was all he thought about every waking moment. He couldn't let her return to New York. He had to convince her to be with him. He was going crazy without her.

He watched her eyes flash as she talked about the kittens in the barn. Her delicate hands motioned as she related Monica's reaction to the baby cats.

His gut clenched at the reminder of the day she'd nearly died. Thankfully, God had intervened and spared her. His chest ached at the loss he'd felt when she'd left and returned to her parents' home. How could he let that happen again?

He'd be so happy if only she'd marry him and move to the farm with Monica. Sweet little Monica who needed a father figure. If only he had the nerve to ask Amanda to stay, his life would be complete.

She'd finished her story about the kittens, but he couldn't remember a thing she'd said.

"Thank you so much for having us here, Bruce." She leaned forward, took both his hands in hers, and kissed his cheek. She was saying good-bye. Tears welled up in his eyes and, through the blur, he threw caution to the wind, grabbed her, and kissed her. Kissed her with all the emotion that had been hidden in his heart. Kissed her with a message of love, longing, and passion.

He held nothing back. If this was good-bye, then he would remember this wild kiss they shared by the water on a blanket in the sunshine.

They parted from the kiss and her eyes were unfocused. She pushed strands of her blonde hair behind her ear. A big diamond winked at him from her ear lobe and he lost his nerve. How could he ask a woman who wore huge diamonds to marry him, a lowly farmer who didn't even know if the farm would show a profit under his management?

AMANDA CAME OUT of the kiss in a place she'd never been before. Her whole world had shifted. Her toes slowly uncurled as she felt the loss of Bruce's heat. She noticed the disconnection almost immediately. She brushed her hair behind her ear and saw that his facial expression changed. Puzzled, she helped tidy the picnic food and garbage away and stood to fold the blanket they'd sat on.

As they rode back to the farm, she tried to figure out what had happened. All the wonderful, passionate feelings she'd experienced moments ago were replaced with a sense of loss. Bruce blasted the radio as if to put distance between them.

AMANDA SPENT THE evening with Nola and Kohkom. Bruce had remained distant since the kiss.

Even though the women had known Matt's death was inevitable, Amanda saw it was something they hadn't been able to prepare for. She remembered the loss and shock of losing Brad. She'd thought because it was sudden that it had been devastating, but now she understood that, even if she'd known it was coming, she could still be in that lonely, desolate place.

Bruce sat on the floor on the far side of the living room playing a game of Candyland with Monica. He was so good with the little ones. He would make a wonderful dad some day.

Her mind drifted back to the picnic. What had happened this afternoon? He had kissed her so passionately then pulled away completely. Did she want to go back to New York where there was no tangible love?

She had a decision to make. Would she leave tomorrow or would she fight for the man she loved? He hadn't asked her to stay. It was up to her to "take the bull by the horns," so to speak.

She put Monica to bed that night with a heavy heart. After checking for monsters and saying prayers, Amanda asked, "Do you like it here?"

Monica's big, round eyes emphasized her sincerity. "Mommy, I like it here. I want to stay."

"Wouldn't you miss our big house in New York and all your cousins?"

"I like it here better, Mommy. The kids and doggies are fun."

Amanda's heart swelled at her daughter's honesty. She liked it here, too.

When she walked into the kitchen after settling Monica in for the night, Bruce was alone, making hot chocolate. He refused to make eye contact with her.

"Bruce, I need to talk to you before I leave. After we have our cocoa, could we take a walk?"

Finally, he turned to meet her gaze. A profound sadness filled his eyes and he nodded.

When they finished their drinks, they excused themselves from the others that had wandered into the kitchen and joined them and walked out to the corral. Bruce hooked his arms over the rail, gazing at the horses. A whirlwind of emotions warred inside Amanda and she swallowed hard.

"Bruce we need to talk." He stood like a statue, unmoving. "You need to look at me, Bruce."

He turned those sad eyes on her. A shiver ran down her spine. "I left you once a few months ago, and it hurt so much." A muscle flexed in his cheek. "I don't want to do it again."

His eyes widened.

"I love you, Bruce Palmer, and I don't want to leave tomorrow."

Several seconds passed. She grabbed hold of his upper arms and pulled him closer so she could see his face better in the yard light. Tears had gathered in his eyes. She sensed the war he fought inside. Heartbreak was a heartbeat away.

Please, Lord, may Your will be done.

His arms came around her. He lifted her and buried his head in the hair at her shoulder. "Buttercup, I can't let you go."

She wrapped her arms around the big, strong man and gave her future to him and to God.

Amanda knew she still had to face testifying at Griffin's trial. Not only that, she'd have to face her mother and her friends and try to explain why she would leave her rich, decadent world for this one.

She had a lot to learn if she became a farmer's wife, but she had a sense that Kohkom and Nola would see her through the learning curve. And it would be worth it all just to be with Bruce for the rest of forever. All she'd ever wanted was a safe home for Monica, a good, caring role model for her father, and a man to protect and love her. In Bruce and the farm at Indian Head, she had found it all. No more running scared.

ABOUT THE AUTHOR

While reading the Internet, Georgina found a quote that said, 'If you write a page everyday you can have a novel in a year.' Well it wasn't that easy. She spent the next four years studying the craft of writing, taking courses and having other writers critique her chapters. While taking a course, she was asked to find three publishers she'd like to submit to. The covers at Prism Book Group drew her in. The rest is history, as they say. *Family Matters,* a story that she had been working on for two years, was contracted. Having conquered sweet romance, she is now working on romantic Christian stories.

Thank you for your Prism Book Group purchase! Visit our website to enjoy free reads, great deals, and entertaining, wholesome fiction!

http://www.prismbookgroup.com

Made in the USA
San Bernardino, CA
16 May 2015